Nurse on
Assignment

Nurse on Assignment

Dorothy Brenner Francis

THORNDIKE
CHIVERS

This Large Print edition is published by Thorndike Press®, Waterville, Maine USA and by BBC Audiobooks Ltd, Bath, England.

Published in 2005 in the U.S. by arrangement with Maureen Moran Agency.

Published in 2005 in the U.K. by arrangement with the author.

U.S. Hardcover 0-7862-8019-0 (Candlelight)
U.K. Hardcover 1-4056-3514-2 (Chivers Large Print)
U.K. Softcover 1-4056-3515-0 (Camden Large Print)

The text of this Large Print edition is unabridged.
Other aspects of the book may vary from the original edition.

Set in 16 pt. Plantin by Liana M. Walker.

Printed in the United States on permanent paper.

British Library Cataloguing-in-Publication Data available

Library of Congress Cataloging-in-Publication Data

Francis, Dorothy Brenner.
    Nurse on assignment / by Dorothy Brenner Francis.
       p. cm. — (Thorndike Press large print Candlelight)
    ISBN 0-7862-8019-0 (lg. print : hc : alk. paper)
    1. Nurses — Fiction. 2. Cayman Islands — Fiction.
I. Title. II. Thorndike Press large print Candlelight series.
PS3556.R327N8685 2005
813'.54—dc22   2005016493

Nurse on Assignment

Chapter One

Linda Carrol ducked into a deserted corridor of Miami General Hospital and pretended to be invisible as she saw Dr. Mercer coming her way. Inhaling the medicinal odor of the surgical center, she held her breath and gazed at an oil seascape hanging near a reception room until the sound of the doctor's footsteps faded away. Then she sighed. She didn't dislike Dr. Mercer, she was just shy about facing anyone whom she didn't know well.

Usually her uniform buoyed her confidence. She felt that everyone respected the nursing profession, and when she donned her white dress and perky cap, it helped her face strangers, supervisors, doctors, patients. Her uniform told everyone that she was Linda Carrol, R.N. R.N. — that was the important thing. When she was in uniform, it didn't matter that she was only

7

five feet tall and rather plain-looking.

But tonight Linda didn't feel like making small talk with anyone. She had been on duty for eight hours, and she had assisted with two appendectomies and two emergencies. There had been no time for a coffee break, and now, since it was eleven p.m., her feet felt like numb stumps and her stomach growled ferociously.

Tossing a pale gold cardigan around her shoulders, Linda stepped out of the hospital into the cool May night. It was only a few steps to the bus stop, but before Linda reached it, a familiar voice hailed her.

"Hi, Blondie! Thought you'd never come off duty! I've been waiting for hours."

Linda hated to be called "Blondie," but her frown disappeared when she looked up into the hazel eyes of Mars Ramsey. For a moment she forgot her weariness. Mars was handsome, and when he was keyed up, as he was now, he hunched his broad shoulders and led with his dark head, and some of his childlike excitement rubbed off on her.

"Mars! You've been here for hours?"

"Well, at least for fifteen minutes." Mars grinned. "It just seems like hours when I'm waiting for you. Come with me, woman — we're going to celebrate!"

Linda noticed now that Mars was wearing his new beige suit and the bright red tie that matched his car.

"Celebrate what? Oh, Mars! You've won a promotion!"

"Well, something like that." Mars took her arm and guided her toward the scarlet convertible parked in the next block. "I've just resigned from Seaside Oil."

"Resigned!" Linda tried to squelch the disappointment from her voice, but when Mars spoke again she knew she had failed.

"Why so glum? Of course I resigned. Seaside Oil had nothing more to offer me. What's the use of hanging on when you've outgrown a job?"

"No use, I suppose," Linda said. She forced herself to say no more. This was the fifth good job that Mars had resigned from in the two years she had known him. Although he had graduated at the top of his college class with a degree in business administration, he flitted from one job to another, always dissatisfied, always searching for something better. And usually he found it. That thought consoled her.

"There was nothing more for me to learn at Seaside, Linda. Nothing. And there was nothing more I could contribute to them. We had reached an impasse."

"You needn't explain."

They had reached his car. He noticed a yellow ticket caught behind the windshield wiper and grabbed it.

"You parked by a fire plug." Linda pointed to the red hydrant.

Mars shrugged as he tore up the ticket. "Guess it didn't matter. There wasn't any fire."

"Mars!" Linda exclaimed. "You can't do that."

"But I just did it." He fluttered the confettied ticket into the gutter and opened the car door for her. "Hop in and decide where we should go. It's a big night! The sky's the limit. Your mother's playing in a film at the Bijou Theater. We could catch the late show."

Linda sighed, knowing that she had to be fresh and rested before she could stand such an ordeal. Even seeing her mother on film made her uneasy. Of course, no one expected her to match her mother's beauty, nor did anyone suspect that she suffered from her own silent comparisons.

Her mother was everything that she was not. Vada met people head on, and they warmed to her immediately. And the same people paid no attention to Linda. As a child she had rubbed vanishing cream on her face and pretended to be invisible. It was a game as well as a protective device. If she were invisible, she wouldn't expect people to notice her, and, by the same token, she wouldn't need to put herself out to notice them.

"I can't go out tonight, Mars." Linda brushed her disturbed feelings aside. "Really I can't."

"You're angry because I resigned. You're angry because I tore up the traffic ticket. Don't be a cube, Linda. Live a little."

Linda had been angry, and she wished she could stay that way. Mars Ramsey could spin her into a state of constant turmoil. But he flashed an instant smile with a sincere friendliness that charmed her out of her negative moods. Somehow a child-like innocence mellowed his aggressiveness, and Linda usually gave in and did as Mars wished. But tonight was different.

"I'm not angry," Linda said. "I'm sorry you've resigned from a perfectly good job, but I'm sure you know what you're doing."

"You bet I do!" Mars thrust the car into gear, and they sped into the stream of traffic flowing toward Linda's apartment. "I've investigated Acme Chemical Company. I know I won't feel restless there. They offer plenty of opportunity for ad-

11

vancement for a creative, progressive thinker. You'll be proud of me, Blondie."

In front of Linda's red brick apartment house Mars slowed the car and grinned at her. "Change into your glad rags and we'll celebrate."

"Mars, I can't. Really. No movie tonight. It's too late."

Mars tilted her chin with the palm of his hand and planted a kiss on her lips. "What were you saying?"

Linda hesitated. "Really, Mars . . . well, maybe there's something else we could do."

"We could get married," Mars suggested. "That's always at the top of my list."

"Be serious." Linda wriggled out of the curve of his arm.

"I am serious. Acme Chemical would look on me with more favor if I were a married man."

"Mars, really! I have to go in." Linda touched the cool metal of the door handle.

"Let's go out to eat," Mars said. "Cicero's. A lobster dinner. The works. Go change."

Mars's infectious manner won out. "How about burgers at Arnold's? I simply can't make a night of it. I have to be back on duty at seven in the morning."

"How come? You just got off duty."

"I promised Betsy North I'd work for her tomorrow. Her mother's sick and she has to fly to Tampa."

"Big-hearted Linda! You pass out the favors, but I'm the one who pays. I was all set to swing."

"I'm sorry," Linda said firmly. "Curfew's at midnight. No later. I can't risk doing a poor job on the floor tomorrow. It wouldn't be fair to my patients or my co-workers."

Without speaking, Mars swung the car into the traffic once more. The parking lot at Arnold's Drive-in was carpeted with wall-to-wall cars, and it was several minutes before a carhop asked for their order.

"Two burgers, two fries, two Cokes." Mars placed the order without consulting Linda. "And make it snappy. Our chariot turns into a pumpkin at midnight."

The carhop gave Mars a quizzical glance, then hurried to relay the order. The odor of hot grease hung on the soft night air, and Linda swatted at a moth that fluttered in front of her nose. Mars was high-handed, but tonight she welcomed the chance to let someone else make her decisions.

"Want the top up?" Mars asked.

"No. I love it this way."

"Arnold's. Moths. Cooking odors. It's so romantic I can hardly bear it. Say you'll be mine."

"Mars, stop clowning!" Linda laughed. "People are staring."

"Let them stare. When are you going to say you'll marry me?"

"I'm only twenty-three. You wouldn't want people to think you had a child bride, would you?" Linda teased, and tried to avoid the subject of marriage. "Here comes our food. I'm famished."

Mars took a sip of his Coke before passing Linda's hamburger and French fries to her. A jukebox blared so loudly that talk was almost impossible, so they ate in silence. After Mars blinked the headlights to signal the carhop to remove their tray, he thrust two dollar bills under his paper cup.

"Lucky carhop," Linda said, eyeing the lavish tip.

"Unlucky Cicero's," Mars replied. "Think of all the money I saved by coming here. I believe in sharing the wealth."

When Mars braked his car in front of Linda's apartment building, she jumped out before he could stop her or persuade

14

her to sit for a while and talk.

"Thanks so much, Mars. Best burger I ever ate."

"I'm flattered," Mars replied with a sigh. "When may I see you again?"

"Why don't you give me a call tomorrow night?" Linda suggested. "I won't be sure of my schedule until then. Okay?"

Mars shrugged as he spurted away from the curb, leaving Linda wondering about his intentions.

She was inside the apartment building and almost to the elevator when she heard her Uncle Sheldon's gravelly voice. Turning, she greeted him with a smile and tried not to show her disapproval of his sneakers, which revealed his big left toe, nor of his black turtleneck sweater that was a relic from his Navy days. She had learned long ago that her uncle valued the old and suspected the new. And he was frugal.

"What on earth are you doing here at this hour, Uncle Sheldon? Is something wrong?"

"Nothing's wrong. It's just that I have a great idea, and it involves you. I couldn't wait another minute to tell you about it and get your reaction. Sit down here in the lobby with me and listen." He pulled a box of raisins from his pocket and offered her some.

Linda shook her head. To her uncle food represented security, and he always carried a little with him. She was amazed that he wasn't fat. Sheldon Burr was tall and bony, and his round face and eyes reminded her of the man in the moon.

Linda sighed again. She was ready to relax. She was always on edge when she was with Mars, always acting the dewy-eyed dream girl that he seemed to expect her to be. With Uncle Sheldon she could be herself.

"What is this fabulous idea that has struck you at the witching hour?" Linda glanced at her watch.

"It didn't just strike me," he replied. "It's just that I've finally worked out all the details. I didn't want to tell you until everything was certain. You see, this idea involves you in a big way. I want you to spend six months with me in the Cayman Islands as my nurse and literary aide."

Linda stared at her uncle, unable to comprehend the magnitude of his suggestion. She knew he had recently recovered from a bout with a bleeding ulcer and that he suffered from chronic bronchitis, but she couldn't imagine that he needed a full-time nurse. And as for being a literary aide, that was completely out of her realm.

"Why are you fleeing to these — islands?" she asked.

"The Cayman Islands," Uncle Sheldon said. "Cayman. You've probably never heard of them. They're sometimes called the 'islands time forgot.' And I'm going there to write about them, of course. That's what a travel writer does, you know. He writes about exotic places. I'm going to put the Caymans in a book for posterity."

"Sounds great," Linda said. "All your books are great. But I don't see how I fit into the picture. Why do you need a nurse?"

"I don't think I do. But Dr. Mercer says I can't go galavanting unless I take one with me. There wouldn't be much for you to do — just plan menus suitable for an ulcer diet and remind me to take my cough pills."

"And who'll prepare your diet food?" Linda asked. "Am I supposed to be cook, too?"

"No, indeed." Uncle Sheldon pulled a travel folder from his inside jacket pocket. "I've written to the managers of the Pirates' Rendezvous — a Mr. and Mrs. McKlintock. They've agreed to rent me a tourist cottage at reduced rates for the off season, and they've promised that their cook will prepare my meals. That's all taken care of. What do you think? Are you interested? I'll pay all expenses, of course, and I'll match whatever salary you're getting at the hospital."

"Where are the Cayman Islands?" Linda asked, stalling. "I've never heard of them."

This time her uncle jerked a map from his pocket. He spread it out between them on the couch and pointed with his bony forefinger.

"The Caymans are a part of the British West Indies. There are three of them — Grand Cayman, Little Cayman, and Cayman Brac. They were first recorded on Columbus' fourth voyage fifteen-oh-three. I plan to stay on Grand Cayman, which is the largest of the group."

Linda peered at the three specks on the map; they were near Jamaica in the Caribbean Sea. "They don't look like much, do they?"

"They're small," he admitted, "but they're beautiful. And I understand that the water surrounding them is so clear that it's a paradise for divers as well as fishermen."

"Who have you talked to?" Linda asked.

"Well, nobody much. Nobody seems to

know a lot about these islands. But I did run into a Caymanian sailor on a small freighter down at the docks, and I've corresponded with the McKlintocks, as I told you. These islands haven't been written about that much. It's a point in their favor as far as I'm concerned."

"They're so small." Linda stalled again. She couldn't quite grasp the idea of abandoning the hospital job, which she loved, to risk six months with her sometimes crotchety uncle on an unheard-of island. But Uncle Sheldon had given her encouragement and moral support during the years after her mother had deserted her for a film career on the continent, those lonely years spent in boarding schools, college, and nurses' training. She owed her uncle a lot, and she was really quite fond of him.

"The islands wouldn't seem small if you could see all of them," he was saying. "They're thought to be just the tips of a drowned mountain range extending from the southern part of Cuba toward the Gulf of Honduras."

"How soon must you have a decision?" Linda stifled a yawn and tried to peek at her watch.

"Take your time, take your time. Tomorrow will be fine. I'd like to be off by the end of the week."

"Tomorrow! End of the week! Uncle Sheldon, even if I decide to go with you, I'll have to give the hospital two weeks' notice. That's an unwritten rule. I'll have a hard time getting a job when I return if I don't play fair now."

Uncle Sheldon sighed. "I suppose you're right. It's just that I'm really excited about this trip. I want to get started as soon as possible now that everything's settled. But I guess I've forgotten to tell you the *real* reason I want to go to the islands."

"You've taken up diving," Linda guessed. "But surely not! Not with your bronchitis."

"No, nothing as rash as all that. But the Cayman Islands used to be the home of the giant green turtles of the Caribbean. I hope to take a trip on a turtle schooner and see first-hand how they catch those giants. Of course, I'd want you to go along to help keep me healthy and organize my notes."

"A turtle schooner?" Linda said. "With sails and spars and all that? Are you sure such things still exist?"

"Maybe not a schooner with sails. But I'm sure the turtlers still exist. The question is, how long will they last? Unless ecologists are successful at saving those creatures, they'll soon pass from the scene, and an epoch will end throughout the Caribbean. This may be my last chance to witness something ancient and wonderful."

"And this is my last chance to get a few winks of sleep before I have to go on duty again," Linda said. "I'm intrigued with your idea, but please let me think it over. I'll give you an answer after work tomorrow. Okay?"

"It's a deal." Uncle Sheldon nodded. "And I hope the answer will be yes. You know I wouldn't have come over here at midnight if this wasn't all-important to me, don't you?"

"I know, and I'm really honored to think you want me to go with you."

It was after one o'clock when Linda's uncle left the building and she went upstairs to her room. Her mind was in a whirl. Mars keyed her up with all his talk of marriage, and now Uncle Sheldon excited her even more with his offer of six months in the Caribbean. Decisions, decisions. But she would decide nothing tonight. Perhaps her brain would function more efficiently in the morning.

Chapter Two

Linda slept restlessly that night, and when she awakened the next morning, her eyelids felt like leather flaps and her brain seemed befogged. It took her a few moments to figure out the reason for the strange sense of apprehension that enveloped her. Uncle Sheldon. The Cayman Islands. Her job.

For a moment she lay there quietly, enjoying the morning glow of her bedroom — sunny yellow walls, saffron draperies, gold carpet. All reflected her usually cheerful disposition.

Slipping from bed, Linda dressed and then prepared toast, cereal, and coffee. As she ate, she tried to reach a decision. She was staring into space, deep in thought, when the intercom buzzed. Her answer was a reflex.

"Hi, Blondie. Spare a cup of coffee for a

poor out-of-work executive?" a familiar voice inquired.

"Mars! Come on up. I've about fifteen minutes before the bus leaves."

"No buses this morning. I'll drive you right to the hospital door."

By the time Linda set out another cup and saucer on a gold place mat, Mars was banging on her door, seemingly unaware that he might be disturbing other tenants with all his noise.

"Come in!" Linda smiled, silently admiring Mars's navy slacks and sport jacket as she closed the door after him.

"If you'd marry me, I wouldn't have to do all this running around for my breakfast," Mars said. "How about it?"

"Mars, Uncle Sheldon was here waiting for me when I got in last night."

"Surely *he* doesn't want to marry you," Mars said, stirring sugar into his coffee. "He's not your type. Too moody."

"Quit clowning and listen to me. Uncle Sheldon has invited me to work for him as his nurse for six months."

"Didn't know he was sick. Looks healthy as a mule — a skinny mule, of course, but healthy."

"He's not really sick. He just has to take care of himself. He's got an ulcer and chronic bronchitis. He's going to the Cayman Islands in the Caribbean to write a book, and Dr. Mercer says he shouldn't go unless a nurse accompanies him."

"You're not seriously considering going, are you?" Mars came to full attention for the first time. "What about me?" He frowned, and his eyebrows looked like two horns where they met over the bridge of his nose.

"As a matter of fact, I am considering going. I've always wanted to travel, and I do like Uncle Sheldon. And this way I wouldn't have to meet so many strangers every day of my life."

"You can run away from me, but you can't run away from yourself, Linda. Don't know why a smooth girl like you is so shy."

"That's easy for you to say. You're the type who's never met a stranger. You don't know what it's like to be afraid you'll be snubbed."

"You go around throwing booby traps in your own path," Mars told her. "Nobody's going to snub you. Anyway, you stick with me and I'll protect you from the hard, cruel world."

"I owe it to Uncle Sheldon to help him out." Linda began rinsing their dishes and stacking them in the sink. "If it weren't for his encouragement and understanding, I wouldn't be wearing this uniform today. He always had time to listen to my troubles and help me find solutions to my problems."

"That dratted uniform makes you too independent," Mars growled. "Stay here with me where you belong."

The more Mars talked the more convinced Linda became that she wanted to give up her job and her apartment. She could stand a little ocean between herself and Mars. The change might give her a new perspective on her personal problems. Did she love him? She knew he wasn't going to give her forever to decide.

"I'm going to tell Mrs. Schrader at the hospital this morning." Linda shuddered at the thought of that confrontation. "Then I'll have to advertise for someone to sublet the apartment. My lease has nine months to run."

Linda stuffed a comb and lipstick into her purse, grabbed a sweater, then locked the apartment door behind them. Mars was silent on the drive to the hospital, and although he had a habit of sulking when he didn't get his own way, Linda couldn't blame him this time. She had a perfectly good job here, and only last night she had criticized him for resigning on a whim.

Mars drove with his broad shoulders squared and his head jutted forward, and he honked impatiently when the car ahead of him was slow to move on the green light. As Linda slammed the car door behind her, she felt as if she were closing the door on their personal relationship. Mars was not one to wait around six months for a frightened rabbit like herself; he would soon be out searching for a nightingale to sing to him throughout the weeks and months.

The familiar hospital odor helped Linda relax, and she found that resigning wasn't as hard as she had thought it might be. Mrs. Schrader accepted her decision with regret, but she wished her well in her new venture. And best of all, she told Linda that if she wanted to, she could leave at the end of the week since someone had applied for a job just two days ago.

"Would this new girl be interested in subletting an apartment?" Linda asked. "She could have mine for six months. It would give her time to look around for a permanent place."

"I'll ask her," Mrs. Schrader said. "I'll let you know tomorrow."

The next few days flew by as quickly as

gulls on the wind. Uncle Sheldon had applauded Linda's decision to accompany him to the Caribbean. Mars had wined and dined her every night, and he had even stopped pleading with her to stay in Miami. And the nurse replacing her had agreed to sublet her apartment. Linda was basking in the warmth of her good fortune when she was summoned to the main desk on her last afternoon at the hospital.

"Dr. Mercer wants to see you before you leave," Mrs. Schrader said. "Better report at once."

"Yes, ma'am." Linda hurried to the rest room, where she freshened her light makeup and ran a comb through her short hair. What could Dr. Mercer want? She barely knew him, and she wondered if she had done something to displease him in these last few harried days.

Gathering her courage, Linda headed for Dr. Mercer's office and tapped gently on the door. At the crisp order to enter, she opened the door and saw the silver-haired doctor sitting behind a huge walnut desk. Cigar smoke curled in a column to join the blue haze near the ceiling, and Dr. Mercer peered at Linda with kindly eyes.

"Miss Carrol, I've been meaning to speak to you about your uncle." Dr.

Mercer came right to the point, and Linda had no time to feel shy or ill at ease.

"He's not the best patient in the world, you know. It's going to be up to you to take care of him while he's off on this wild chase. Green turtles! Who'd believe it?"

"He's a writer," Linda said, as if that explained everything.

"I want you to prepare a first-aid kit to take with you," Dr. Mercer said. "There's a small hospital on Grand Cayman, but I want you to be equipped with some emergency items, along with a full supply of your uncle's regular medicines."

"What shall I include in the kit?" Linda asked, reaching into her purse for pencil and paper. "The usual?"

Dr. Mercer nodded. "Some one-inch adhesive dressings and some of medium size. You can also put in the large size. Better include plenty of insect repellent, ointment for burns, antiseptics, and some triangular bandages. A tourniquet might come in handy. These things are basic. I'll give you some prescriptions for his ulcer condition and for some antibiotics. He's fighting a stubborn bronchial infection. Some of these antibiotics work against his ulcer, so I'll include instructions for rotating them."

"Shall I pack a vaporizer?" Linda asked.

"No need," Dr. Mercer replied. "It's a humid climate."

He wrote out the prescriptions, then looked up at Linda with a smile. "Keep Sheldon from overdoing it. He frequently overestimates his strength, and too much activity aggravates his cough. Do his errands for him whenever you can, and don't forget to dispense large doses of TLC."

"Tender, loving care?"

"Right. His active imagination can turn a minor illness into a chronic one. As successful a writer as he is, he worries about his work. Worry and apprehension can make him ill, but cheerfulness can make him well. You've shown many instances of having a clear insight into patients' psychological problems. That's why I recommended you to Sheldon for this job. That you are his niece is purely coincidental."

"I'll be sympathetic to his needs," Linda promised, amazed that Dr. Mercer had actually noticed her.

"No. Sympathy is the last thing he needs when he's really sick. When he's ill, he's gloomy and responds poorly to positive statements about his health. Of course, he'll think you're unkind for not sympathizing, but you'll have to be firm. The best medicine is preventive medicine.

"Your uncle tends to let negative thoughts bring on illness, but he can create miracles of self-healing if there's someone around to help keep him serene. You'll be smart to supply cheerfulness, optimism, and laughter in large daily doses. This is why I insisted on his taking a nurse with him, a nurse who understands him. He has no business going on such a trip alone. I have every confidence that you'll keep him in top condition until I see him six months from now."

"Thank you, Dr. Mercer."

"And incidentally, Miss Carrol, if you do a good job on this assignment, I'm sure more special-duty work will come your way. I'm not sure you were cut out to be a floor nurse. Your supervisor has told me how difficult it is for you to meet people. She even asked for your dismissal, but I thought that unfair. I believe you may blossom as a private-duty nurse."

"Thank you for the advice and the pre-scriptions, Dr. Mercer," Linda said. "I'll do my best for Uncle Sheldon, for both of you."

She felt her face flaming as she left the doctor's office. She had had no idea that she was about to be dismissed. But now she remembered how willingly her resignation had been received. How lucky she was that Dr. Mercer had given her another chance to prove her worth!

Assembling the items for her first-aid kit filled most of the rest of her day. After having talked to Dr. Mercer, her job took on more importance. The fact that her uncle's health and well-being depended so much on her actions and attitudes was a bit frightening. But it was also challenging, and she knew she mustn't fail either Uncle Sheldon or herself.

That evening Linda packed the things she planned to take with her. And the following morning she was waiting in the apartment lobby for over fifteen minutes before her uncle came by in a taxi.

"Uncle Sheldon! I'm so excited I hardly slept a wink all night, and I couldn't eat a thing this morning."

After loading her luggage into the taxi, her uncle gave orders to the cab driver, then turned to Linda, his moonlike face bright with eagerness.

"You're no more excited than I am. I only wish we could have traveled by boat."

"You dislike flying?" Linda asked.

"Not really." He glanced down at his tight leather shoes and shrugged his bony shoulders under his sport coat. "It's just that I could have worn my old comfortable clothes if we had traveled by tramp steamer. There're some small trading vessels out of Tampa, but they're unscheduled, and I'm eager to reach our destination."

After a short ride to the airport, Linda and her uncle boarded a small Lacsa Airline plane that flew from Miami to the Cayman Islands and then on to Central America. The plane was dwarfed by larger jets on the airstrip, and somehow Linda didn't feel as if their reservations were confirmed until they snapped their seat belts into place.

The smell of diesel exhaust seeped into the plane, and Linda felt her feet tingle as the vibrations of the engines shook the floorboards. The plane taxied down the airstrip for takeoff, and for a moment Linda felt as if unseen hands were pressing her against the seat cushion. Then they were airborne and she relaxed.

During the flight Uncle Sheldon chatted endlessly about his plans for a book about the Caymans, and Linda listened with unfeigned interest. The stewardess served them a light lunch, and almost before she had removed their trays, they received orders to fasten their seat belts for landing.

Linda peered out of her window. From this height it was easy to guess the depth of the water beneath them. The cobalt-blue color indicated the deep water of the open sea, the purple-brown shades bespoke of coral heads, and the yellowish tint denoted a sandy bottom.

Their touchdown at Georgetown was smooth, and Linda smiled in pleasure as they stepped from the plane into the damp warmth of the tropics. A gentle trade wind blew her hair back from her face, and she could almost taste the sea salt in the sultry air. As they walked across the airstrip to the terminal building she saw a tall, sandy-haired young man approaching them at a leisurely pace. He was dressed simply in white sneakers and fresh khakis, but his features were so sharp and fine that his profile reminded Linda of the likeness of a Roman Caesar cut on a gold coin. Only his eyes bespoke a dreamy quality that didn't seem to match the rest of him.

"You must be Mr. Sheldon Burr and Miss Linda Carrol," the young man said. "Welcome to Grand Cayman. I'm Duncan McKlintock. My friends all call me Klint. My parents operate the Pirates' Rendez-vous, and I'm their official greeter."

Grahn Caymahn. Linda repeated the

words to herself. The boy spoke with a burr that sounded almost Scottish, yet his words sang with a calypso rhythm that fascinated her.

Uncle Sheldon took over the conversation. Linda hardly had a chance to say a word, and she was glad. Klint was so handsome that he left her speechless. At least that was what she tried to tell herself. It was really her same old shyness that left her speechless, but now she felt no desire to be invisible.

They picked up the luggage and then loaded it into a strange-looking car that appeared to be going downhill even while it was standing still.

"It's French," Klint said in response to Linda's quizzical glance at the car.

Linda still said nothing, but once they were in the car, she gasped in surprise as Klint drove off on the left-hand side of the road.

"It's like in England," Uncle Sheldon explained. "The islands are British, you know."

Linda was a bit disappointed in the scenery that surrounded her. There were no dramatic mountains to form a backdrop for a romantic setting. There was no great profusion of flowers, no meandering rivers or dense tropical jungles. But the sand on the beach was the whitest she had ever seen, and it pointed up the brilliance of the blue sky and the sea.

"Grand Cayman is about twenty-three miles from west to east," Klint said, sounding like a tour guide as they drove through a swampy mangrove and buttonwood area. "And its widest spot measures about eight miles. This Great North Sound almost cuts the island in two. Now, the trees on your right are breadfruit and tropical almond. And, of course, you probably recognize the bougainvillaea vines and the palmettos."

"I understand that most of the tourists have gone home," Uncle Sheldon said.

"Right," Klint agreed. "The winter months comprise our tourist season. The summer humidity and the mosquitoes are too much for most people. You'll meet a few hardy souls at the lodge, though. Miss Carrol, you'll enjoy shopping while you're here. Grand Cayman now has free-port status. You can buy English China, French perfume, and cameras at very reasonable prices. There are some unique shops in Georgetown."

"Thank you," Linda replied. "It sounds very interesting." How could she sound so dull! Better to keep quiet than to make a fool of herself.

"How much farther?" Uncle Sheldon asked.

"Just a few miles," Klint said. "We're located on Seven-Mile Beach at West Bay. The beach is a graceful curve of sand, really about five miles long, but we try to please the tourists. It was called Six-Mile Beach until just a few years ago. It's north of Georgetown on the island's western face."

After a few minutes Klint turned onto a narrow lane that led to the Pirates' Rendezvous. It consisted of a series of pastel-colored cottages with airy screened-in porches facing the Caribbean. A central lodge with a sitting porch, a dining hall, and a kitchen formed the hub of the complex; oleander, hibiscus, and bougainvillaea abounded.

"Oh, what a beautiful ship!" Linda exclaimed as she caught sight of white sails against the azure sky.

"That's the *Hawksbill*," Klint said. "It's a schooner patterned after the old turtle boats of bygone years. I built it in my spare time."

"Built it!" Linda leaned forward for a closer look. "It's beautiful. Does it work? I mean, do you take it out on the sea?"

"She's seaworthy," Klint said. "Stands up to her cloth real well. She's quite a tourist attraction in season. I'll take you for a sail before you leave here."

He stopped the car in front of a pink cottage and helped them carry their luggage inside. Then he turned to leave.

"What about a key?" Uncle Sheldon asked.

Klint shrugged. "No locks on the doors. Guess we could install one for you if you'd like. Most of our visitors don't feel the need for one. We have no poverty, no begging, no major crimes."

"Let it go." Uncle Sheldon dismissed Klint with a nod, and to Linda's surprise she agreed with him. There was a serenity about the island that made locks and keys seem superfluous.

Chapter Three

The bare tile floors and bamboo furniture of the cottage gave the impression of airy spaciousness. Linda's room, done in icy blues and greens, was like an extension of the sea, and her uncle's room, with its sand tones sparked with splashes of orange, was restful and inviting. Someone had placed a single green orchid in the crystal dish on Linda's desk, and she could hardly believe it was real.

While hanging her clothes in the closet, Linda wondered if three uniforms would be enough to see her through six months' duty. Perhaps she should have brought four to have been on the safe side. She slid her first-aid kit into the closet, then, thinking better of it, pulled it out and placed it on a straight chair near the desk. She would be using her portable hospital every day, and she wanted to keep it handy.

After Linda had finished unpacking, she heard her uncle coughing, and she tapped on the door between their rooms.

"Are you okay, Uncle Sheldon?" She peeked into his room and saw him jackknifed in a spasm of coughing. She made him sit down and brought him a glass of water.

"Hope I'm not going to have a bout of coughing first thing here," Uncle Sheldon wheezed.

"Of course you're not," Linda assured him in her best bedside manner. "You've had a hard day and you need rest. This tropical humidity should ease your cough. I can understand why Dr. Mercer said I didn't need to bring a vaporizer."

"I'm starving," Uncle Sheldon said when his coughing subsided. "Could we splurge and have a square meal for a change?"

Linda shook her head. "Now, you're not going to give me a bad time about the diet, are you? You know you're better off when you eat several small meals rather than a large one."

Linda won out. They rested a while, then ate a bland meal in their rooms. Linda was too tired to take a walk that evening, and she hoped the tropical climate wasn't going to make her lethargic. She went to bed early, and after her uncle stopped puttering around with books, papers, and typewriter, she was able to listen to the night sounds of Grand Cayman. The surf with its steady pulsing, the breeze that whispered through the almond tree outside her window, the sound of guitar music and voices from the dining hall.

A mosquito singing near her left ear awakened Linda the next morning, and she began her day by anointing herself with insect repellent. As soon as she was dressed in her uniform, she knocked on her uncle's door. She had heard him moving about for some time.

"Come on in, Linda."

"Brought you some Bug-a-Boo." Linda plunked the tube of ointment on her uncle's desk. "These mosquitoes are going to be pesky."

Her uncle applied some repellent to his neck and ears, and Linda smiled as a mosquito lit on a patch of bare skin that showed through a hole in his T-shirt. But her smile vanished when her uncle spoke.

"One thing, Linda. No uniforms while we're here. Never thought to mention it to you before. But they won't be necessary."

"Oh, I don't mind wearing my uniform," Linda said. "It'll be no trouble at all."

"You misunderstand me." Uncle Sheldon wiggled the toe that poked through his worn sneaker, and his voice took on a stern quality. "I don't *want* you to wear a uniform. You're a secret-assignment nurse. The McKlintocks and their staff know I have some minor health problems, but I don't want anyone to get the impression that I'm an invalid, that I'm an old man. You can do your Flo Nightingale bit just as efficiently in plain clothes and on the q.t. I intend to introduce you as my literary aide. I did mention that beforehand, you know."

"I know." Linda's thoughts tumbled over themselves until she could hardly think clearly. "But since I'm not a literary person, I thought you had to be kidding. I can't write."

"You won't need to. At least not much. I want you to mingle with people and keep a mental antenna alert for human interest stories that I might miss."

"Uncle Sheldon! You know I'm no good at approaching strangers. I just — well, I just can't do it."

Uncle Sheldon drew himself up to his full height and stared down at her. "Emerson said, and I quote, 'He has not learned the lesson of life who does not

41

every day surmount a fear.' Roughly translated, that means if approaching strangers scares you, approach them, anyway. Now change your clothes and we'll go to breakfast."

Linda fled to her room to squelch the tears that were stinging her eyelids. No uniform! Six months with no uniform! And her uncle expected her to seek out strangers, to draw stories from them. Didn't he know that without her uniform she was nothing? Why hadn't she stayed in Miami, where she was sure of Mars's company? She could stand some of his protection right now.

Somehow Linda managed to change into a blue skimmer and sandals, and when she and her uncle reached the dining room, she tried to forget her troubles as Mr. and Mrs. McKlintock greeted them.

The dining area was really a large screened-in porch with a bare planked floor and a rough-beamed ceiling. All the dining tables were arranged so that their occupants would have an ocean view as they sat in chairs fashioned after rum kegs. Around the edge of the room were placed iron-bound pirates' chests, serving as occasional chairs or magazine stands.

The McKlintocks were a middle-aged

couple, both blue-eyed, sandy-haired, and sun-weathered. Linda guessed that they had lived in the relative seclusion of their island paradise for so long that they had grown to look alike. They even wore identical flowered shirts over gleaming white slacks.

"Oh, we're Scottish," Mrs. McKlintock said in answer to Uncle Sheldon's question.

"Our ancestors fled here during Cromwell's revolution in the British Isles," Mr. McKlintock added. "The population of the Caymans is about one-third white, one-third black, and one-third in between. The most cosmopolitan group you'll find anywhere."

"Racial problems?" Uncle Sheldon asked.

The McKlintocks shook their heads. "Everyone's color-blind. White, black, or otherwise, we're all Caymanians."

Mrs. McKlintock nodded toward the kitchen. "Come meet our cook and her helper. They're lovely women, and they'll be instrumental in making your stay here pleasant. There's a bit of rivalry between them over their cooking abilities, but nothing serious. The end result is tip-top meals."

Linda and her uncle followed the McKlintocks to the spotlessly clean kitchen, where they were introduced to Virgie Wonder, the head cook, and her helper, Gem Smith. Virgie wore a slightly worried expression as she smoothed her white apron and primped at her hair. She studied them for a moment, then with plump arms akimbo she blurted, "You de ulcer patient?"

"I do have a stomach problem," Uncle Sheldon admitted, his round face flushing. "But it's under control at the moment."

"Virgie keep it under control. You no worry about dat." Virgie's weather-seamed face flushed with pleasure, and her blue eyes sparkled with intelligence.

"And this is Gem —" Mrs. McKlintock's voice broke off as the cook's helper interrupted her.

"I saw you arrive yesterday." Gem spoke so fast that her words tumbled over one another. "Never before do I meet a famous author. Never before." Gem's hands fluttered as she toyed with a gold coin suspended on a chain around her neck.

In spite of Gem's dark coloring, she reminded Linda of quicksilver. She moved fast, she talked fast, and her eyes darted here and there like birds. She gave the im-

44

pression of flying even though she was standing still.

After Linda and her uncle had returned to their table, Mrs. McKlintock filled them in on the two women they had just met.

"Virgie's English. Claims to be a descendant of Henry Morgan, the pirate. Her husband deserted her, and now she keeps house for her brother-in-law, Captain Taurus Gibraltar, when he's not turtling. She's an outspoken perfectionist, and she and Taurus sometimes tangle, but they're good for each other."

"This Captain Taurus Gibraltar," Uncle Sheldon said, immediately alert, "does he hunt the green turtles?"

"That's right," Mr. McKlintock said. "He's been out since mid-April. He may be back the end of this month or the first of June. It'll be a sight to see them unload the turtles into the crawls."

"Any chance he'd go out again?" Uncle Sheldon asked. "I don't think my book would be complete without an eyewitness account of a turtle voyage."

Mr. McKlintock shook his head and shrugged. "Hard to say what Captain Taurus will or won't do. He's a stubborn one."

"There's a rock in the Mediterranean

45

named after him," Mrs. McKlintock said with a laugh. "But you might work at it through Virgie. Sometimes Taurus will do for her what he wouldn't do for anyone else."

"She seems persuasive," Uncle Sheldon said.

"Persuasive!" Mr. McKlintock slapped his knee. "Taurus gives in to her just to hush her up. Says he can't stand a woman with a tent-flap mouth."

"Tell us about Gem," Linda said, surprised at her own boldness. "She looks as if she might be Indian."

"Right," Mrs. McKlintock said. "That brown skin and broad, lean face are unmistakable indications. Gem comes from a turtling family from Nicaragua. She's a bit flighty, but indispensable."

When Virgie served breakfast, the McKlintocks excused themselves and left. Linda wondered where Klint was, but she didn't voice the question. Instead, she listened to her uncle's plans for the day.

"Thought we'd take a long hike right after breakfast," he said. "Best way to see a place is on foot. I'll ask Virgie to pack us a lunch. You can suggest the menu, but I'll give the orders. Okay?"

Linda nodded and jotted down suggestions for lunch on a scrap of paper from her purse.

Their day of exploring was pleasant but tiring. Linda tried to hold her uncle to a slow pace. She listened patiently as he pointed out almond trees, mangrove swamps, bougainvillaea vines, and other flora of the island. They tramped along the beach and trudged inland through scrub forests. They swatted mosquitoes and emptied sand from their shoes. Linda wondered how her uncle could resist taking a swim, but he did.

When they returned to their cottage, Linda was too tired to swim. Even her uncle was content to rest until dinnertime, when he appeared in his well-ventilated sneakers and a tattered T-shirt.

"Shouldn't we dress for dinner?" Linda protested.

"I'll have my meal sent here," Uncle Sheldon replied. "I'm really bushed. And I want to go over the notes I took today and file them in order. You go ahead to the dining room. Have them send me whatever you please. And you might try to get on the good side of Virgie. She may be our key to a turtle voyage."

Linda considered having her own dinner sent to the cottage, then she thought better

47

of it. Uncle Sheldon would be working, so she might as well go out and enjoy the tropical evening. She hadn't even had time to inspect Mrs. McKlintock's orchid beds around the dining hall, and she had noticed their beauty that morning. But she had no intention of approaching Virgie with a request for a turtle hunt.

After changing into a peppermint-striped dress, Linda strolled to the dining room. Gem took her order and flew to fill it as if she had wings on her heels. Linda had chosen an out-of-the-way table that overlooked the sea, and she saw Klint enter the hall before he saw her. He still reminded her of a Caesar, and her heart beat faster as he noticed her and strode directly to her table.

"May I join you?" he asked. "You're gazing at the ocean as if you're dreaming of Spanish galleons and pirate ships."

Linda nodded. "How did you guess? I hear that Henry Morgan slept here."

Klint grinned. "And Edward Teach, better known as Blackbeard. Some of our pirate chests may have belonged to those two. They were salvaged on the reef. Where have you been hiding all day?"

"Uncle Sheldon and I took a hike." Linda stated the plain fact and felt herself blush when she could think of nothing more to say. Her words froze in her throat, although she longed to ask more about the pirate chests.

"No swimming?" Klint asked.

"Not today. But I love to swim. I even brought fins and a mask and a snorkel." Linda immediately wished she could snatch those words back. Surely Klint would think she was hinting.

"What are you having to eat?" Klint asked. "Going to try our green turtle steak?"

"I ordered a fruit plate. The thought of eating turtle —"

Linda relaxed when her meal arrived. Klint couldn't expect her to talk and eat at the same time, and she was quite contented to let him talk and entertain her the way Mars had always done.

Klint looked over the other diners and pointed out a group of marine archaeologists who had just arrived from Jamaica, where they had been exploring the sunken ruins of Port Royale, an ancient pirate hangout.

"They're trying to build a scientific picture of what the old port was like, but I suspect they're like little kids trying to figure out an intriguing puzzle."

"Who are the men at that table in the corner?" Linda asked.

"That's an entomology team from the U.S. They're here to study and try to conquer our mosquito problem. And they're sincere in their work. I've talked to each of them. They're experimenting with all sorts of tests. If we had a few less mosquitoes and a few more men, Grand Cayman would indeed be a paradise for young lady vacationers."

"Why more men?" Linda asked, wondering if Klint always analyzed everyone's motives as he had those of the entomology team and the salvage divers. "Is there a man shortage?"

"Most of the local boys leave home and go to sea on freighters or tankers," Klint explained. "Caymanian sailors are noted for their outstanding seamanship, and they have no trouble getting good jobs. Our seamen, our good turtle years, and our tourists keep us prosperous. Of course, the stamp sale helps, too."

"What kind of stamps?" Linda tasted a mango, then took a sip of tea.

"Postage stamps. I'll have to show you my collection before you leave here. Our stamps have always been collector's items, and in part they were designed for that. In nineteen hundred King George the Sixth was crowned, and our coronation stamp issue had a great sale. The profits contributed to the construction of lighthouses, a library, and a small hospital."

"I'd like to see the hospital," Linda said.

"Feeling ill?"

"I'm a nurse." Linda blurted the information before she had time to think. "I'm just taking a few months off to help my uncle with his work," she said quickly. "Do you think there's any chance that Captain Gibraltar will take him out on a turtle voyage?"

Klint shrugged. "Captain Taurus is mule-stubborn. It's hard to predict what his reaction to such a request would be. But with him, money talks. If your uncle's willing to pay a 'faht fee,' Captain Taurus might be persuaded. The turtles have been gone from here for two hundred years, you know. It's rather sad when you think that the island used to abound with them."

"I didn't know," Linda said. "Where are the turtles now? Where has the captain gone?"

"He sails to the Miskito Bank near Nicaragua for his hunts," Klint told her. "It's about three or four hundred miles from here. But if he sailed out again in June, he would have to travel even farther south. What are you going to do here for six months? You'll surely be bored to death."

"I'll take care of my uncle," Linda replied, again without thinking.

"Take care of him? Is he sick?"

"Oh, not really." Linda tried to cover her blunder. She had supposed that Klint's parents had told him about Uncle Sheldon. "At least don't hint to him that I said he was. He just has this ulcer that needs to be babied. I'm really supposed to be helping him with his writing."

"How? Typing?"

"He wants me to help him collect local-color stories," Linda said glumly. "And I know I can't do it. It's impossible. I simply can't face strangers and start a conversation. The thought of being snubbed chills me."

"What makes you think you'll be snubbed? Caymanians are friendly people. You'll enjoy them."

"But will they enjoy me? That's the big question."

"I do," Klint said simply. "I enjoy you very much. I barged right over to you and sat down and began talking. Why didn't you snub me?"

Linda was quiet for so long that Klint

spoke again. "Don't tell me you're going to start snubbing now?"

Linda laughed. "Of course not. I was just trying to find the answer to your question. Why didn't I snub you? I guess it was because I sensed that you approached me with an honest desire to be friendly."

"Right," Klint agreed. "I used to be shy myself, until I realized that some of my best friends were once strangers."

"Maybe some of your bravery will rub off on me," Linda said.

"Nothing brave about it. New people are no more dangerous than familiar people, and sometimes they're a lot more exciting."

Linda had to agree. Although she had met Klint only a short time ago, she knew already that he was one of the most exciting people she had ever known. It startled her to realize that she had hardly given Mars a thought in the last twenty-four hours.

"How would you like to meet Virgie?" Klint asked. "She's a good one for starters. She likes everyone."

"Your mother introduced me to her this morning."

"I mean really meet her," Klint said. "Tomorrow's her day off. Mom and Gem manage the dining hall. How about going with me to visit Virgie at her home? I'll get her okay. That'll be no problem. We could rent bicycles, take a lunch, and make a day of it, if you'd like. You could talk to her about anything you want."

"I'd love to go," Linda answered. "If it's okay with Uncle Sheldon, of course."

"Tell him the visit would be to his advantage," Klint said. "That's why I suggested Virgie. Get on the good side of her, and she'll plug for you all the way. And she's quite influential with Captain Taurus."

"I wouldn't want her to feel that I was using her," Linda said.

"A person knows when another person is truly interested in him. Virgie won't be fooled. Is it a date?"

Linda nodded, and when she rose to leave the dining room, Klint said he would walk her back to her cottage. They had talked for so long that darkness had fallen. Birds twittered a muted night song, and an insect chorus tuned up, ready to serenade. There was little twilight on Grand Cayman. Once the sun sank below the horizon, a velvet darkness cloaked the island. But Linda didn't mind. She felt safe and at ease with Klint.

Chapter Four

When Linda tapped on her uncle's door the following morning, all was quiet. She knocked again. No answer.

"Uncle Sheldon?" Linda called, and opened the door a crack. Then she opened it wide and strode inside. Her uncle was sitting in a chair with a glazed expression on his face.

"What's the matter?" Linda asked. "Are you ill?" She felt a rising panic and wished that she had curtailed more of her uncle's activities the day before. Her uncle glanced at her as if he were seeing her for the first time. Then he sighed.

"Of course I'm not ill. I'm just discouraged. These islands! These people!" He nodded toward a ream of paper stacked by his typewriter. "It's all so wonderful and marvelous that I'll never catch it all on paper. Never."

Linda was alert to her uncle's depressed mood as she brought him his antibiotic and a glass of water. "You've always managed to get it all down on paper in the past. Why should this time be different? Your book on Australia was on the bestseller list for weeks. Remember?"

"So it was. So it was." Uncle Sheldon swallowed his capsule and stared toward the sea.

"What would you like to eat today?" Linda smiled as she sat down to prepare the day's menu, but her cheerfulness wasn't contagious.

"You talk as if I have a choice."

"Of course you have a choice. You know that. You just have to be careful, that's all. How about cereal, toast, and tea for breakfast?"

"Yeah! That's real different."

"And for lunch you could have a mild clam chowder and a gelatin salad, or maybe a custard."

"I'm thrilled." Uncle Sheldon began pacing the floor.

"Well, here's something different. Klint — Duncan McKlintock — says they're serving green turtle steak and that it's great. He says it's like veal. I think you could have a small portion of that."

"Just what I've always wanted — green turtle steak."

"You really should know what it tastes like if you're going to describe it for your readers." Linda was careful to squelch the irritation that threatened to tinge her voice. Then she remembered her plans for the day. "Uncle Sheldon! I forgot to tell you. Guess what Klint has invited me to do today?"

"Get married? Oh, no, that's Mars's line. What does Duncan McKlintock have in mind?"

"If it's all right with you, we're going to bicycle to Virgie's home and visit with her. It's her day off, and Klint's going to make all the arrangements."

For the first time that morning Uncle Sheldon's expression brightened, and his voice lost its gravel-slide quality. "I knew you could do it, Linda. You hang right in there. Don't take a notebook or anything like that. Might scare her, but you remember every word she says. Write me a synopsis the minute you get back. And it wouldn't hurt a thing to work the conversation around to Captain Taurus Gibraltar, if you know what I mean."

"Uncle Sheldon!" Linda almost regretted her decision to go with Klint. She was proud to have pulled her uncle from his gloomy mood, but now she had put herself on the spot.

During breakfast she hardly spoke. To fail her uncle would be to fail herself, and she felt inadequate to meet his demands. She sat where she could watch the surf scallop the white beach, and gradually the endless flow of water had a soothing effect on her. After she ate she returned to her room. She had thought she was ready to go bicycling, but now she criticized herself in the mirror.

What would Klint expect her to wear? What would he like her to wear? Suddenly, pleasing Klint rated top priority in her mind, and she tried on three outfits before deciding on the gold pantsuit that matched her hair and the blue sleeveless shell that accented her eyes.

When Klint arrived, he visited with Linda's uncle for a few minutes. His no-hurry attitude pleased Linda. At last they strolled to a bicycle rental stall that was situated in the shade of some breadfruit trees and was managed by a dark-skinned boy who was idly strumming a guitar.

Linda hung back and let Klint do all the talking, and in a few minutes they were bicycle-bound for Virgie's cottage. Klint pedaled with an easygoing grace, and when the wind ruffled his sandy hair, he reminded her of a small boy staring dreamily at the sea.

"How far to Virgie's?" Linda asked.

"Several miles. I've brought along a lunch to share with her." Klint tapped a cardboard box that he had placed in the bicycle basket, then his eyes went back to the sea. Linda followed his gaze.

"What do you see out there?" Klint asked.

"Water," Linda answered. "What do you see?"

"I see the *Hawksbill* under full sail heading back from Miami with a load of tourists seeking adventure on the high seas and a welcome on these islands."

"Do you really plan to sail your schooner clear to Miami? Would it be possible?"

"It would be possible, but not practical." When Klint smiled at her, deep lines fanned out from his sea-blue eyes. "I'd like to start a boat service between the Caymans and Miami. People have tried it before and failed, but I think I could make a success of it. But no sails. People don't have time for that kind of voyage these days. It's really too bad."

"Your schooner is like a dream from a

59

storybook world. People will love it." Linda was surprised to see Klint's ears turn pink, and it thrilled her to know that she had pleased him with her comment.

"Tell me about your life as a nurse," Klint said. "Where did you work?"

Linda told him about Miami General and about many of her experiences there before she realized that she was doing all the talking. Klint had a way of listening that made you believe he was truly interested, but she wondered if he was analyzing her. When she realized that she was monopolizing the conversation, she tried to shift the talk to him.

"What do you do on Grand Cayman all year long?"

"Just this and that," Klint said. "I built the *Hawksbill* last year. During the tourist season the folks need an extra hand around the lodge."

Linda asked more questions, but she felt that Klint's answers were guarded. Somehow he had managed to find out a lot more about her than she had found out about him. They were both staring at the sea once more as they rounded a curve in the road and saw a man neck-deep in the water of a quiet cove. Two other men sat in a catboat nearby.

"Git de big one, Kimo," one of the boatmen yelled.

"What are they doing?" Linda asked as Klint stopped his bike to watch them.

"We're just in time to see Kimo bring a turtle out of the crawl. Probably the one Gem's going to serve for dinner tonight at the lodge."

"How does he know there's a turtle there?"

"Because Captain Taurus released his catch there after one of his turtling voyages. The crawls are underwater corrals. Mangrove stakes are used to make huge square pens under the water. You can see them sticking above the surface like spikes." Klint pointed. "The stakes are lashed together with thatch rope so that the turtles can't escape."

"That man's in there with those huge creatures?" Linda shuddered. "Isn't that dangerous?"

Klint laughed. "They're vegetarians."

The man called Kimo took a dive, and soon the water was churned into a white froth. He surfaced holding a huge turtle in front of him in a bear hug; then man and turtle disappeared beneath the sea. The next time they surfaced, the man held the turtle by a rope that formed a bridle around its front flippers.

"How did he do that?" Linda gasped.

"Underwater he grasps the turtle by the shell behind its head, then slips the ropes over the front flippers to form a sort of harness. Now they'll haul it into the cat-boat."

Linda wished she had brought a note-book. Surely Uncle Sheldon would be interested in this! And just as surely she would forget some of the details. But she would remember the fierce look of the dark-skinned native, pompous in his strength as the water frothed about him, and she would never forget the sight of the huge green turtle as it thudded into the catboat. She tried to memorize the living-reptile odor of the sea, and the sound of the surging water slapping against the boat and drowning out the shouts of the men.

"Want a close-up?" Klint asked. Then, not waiting for her answer, he motioned her to bike nearer to the shore.

"She be big," one of the men shouted to Klint as they drew near.

Linda watched the sun play on the brown-skinned men as they glided through the water. They seemed almost an extension of their craft, so sure and easy were their movements. After they pulled the boat ashore, Linda peered into it. The turtle lay on its back with a block of wood supporting its head.

"Its own weight would suffocate it if they placed it right side up," Klint told her.

"It's crying." Linda pointed to tears that squeezed from the creature's eyes.

"Turtles don't cry," Klint assured her. "That's lubricating fluid that helps their eyelids to function."

Klint spoke with the men for a few minutes before they pulled away from shore; then Linda and Klint continued on their way.

"I wish Uncle Sheldon could have seen that," Linda said as they pedaled along. "I'll never be able to tell it as well as he could. He has a way of writing that makes people feel what he feels."

"Maybe he can come here sometime and see the boys bring out a big one. It's not as if it were a one-time thing, you know. Turtle meat, turtle soup, they're a common part of our diet."

They rode on in a comfortable silence, and Linda relaxed. It was nice not to have to be "on" every second of the time. She was glad they had seen the men bringing in the turtle. At least she would have that to tell Uncle Sheldon, even if she failed to learn anything interesting from Virgie.

Linda panted as they pumped uphill. She hadn't noticed when they left the mangrove swamps behind, but now they were on higher ground that was punctuated by gray limestone outcroppings and a kind of tree that Klint called a gumbo-limbo.

"They're beautiful," Linda said. "Unique."

"I suppose so," Klint replied. "I guess I'm so used to them that I don't really see them."

"When the sun is caught in those peels of shedding bark, they look copper-colored, almost translucent. They really seem rather eerie against this sable landscape. Why is everything so black?"

"It's farmland that's been burned over. One journalist described those gumbo-limbos as 'the torches of hell.' You might tell that to your uncle. There's an area here called Hell. It's got a post office so that tourists can send wish-you-were-here cards to their friends."

They pedaled on over a trail that was white and sandy. The fields were fenced with limestone cobbles that, Linda guessed, had been stacked by hand. Inside the fences a few cattle and an occasional horse grazed. They were quite a distance

64

inland when they came to Virgie's home, which sat at the end of a narrow lane.

The small frame house was painted a light blue, and a tall mango tree shaded it from the sun. They had barely propped their bicycles on their brake stands when Virgie's plump form filled the doorway. Smoothing her hair with one hand, she held the screen wide with the other and invited them inside.

"We've come to share our lunch with you," Klint said by way of greeting. "You remember Linda Carrol, don't you?"

"Of course," Virgie replied. "I be working in my garden, but now I rest. I make a cool drink."

"Fine," Klint said. "We'll have it with our lunch."

Linda's mouth felt like dry wool, and she didn't know if it was from their long ride or from her fear of facing Virgie at such close range. She was glad that Klint carried the conversational ball.

Virgie's house was small, but it was as clean and neat as the kitchen at the Pirates' Rendezvous. Rag rugs dotted the bare floor, and lacy curtains hung at the windows. Virgie spread a starched white cloth over a small table in the main room, which served as a sitting and dining room. Then she brought out pale blue plates and went into the kitchen. Klint opened the lunch box and placed a wedge of cheese, a loaf of unsliced bread, and a bunch of bananas on the table.

"Virgie," he called, "we'll need a knife."

When Virgie returned with the knife, Klint acted as host, serving generous portions of the lunch he had provided. Clearly, Virgie enjoyed the food, and Linda couldn't blame her. Never had such simple fare tasted so good. For a while they were so busy eating that conversation lagged, but at last Linda knew she had to say something.

"You have a beautiful home, Virgie," she commented.

"I thank you," Virgie said. "It pleases de captain and myself."

Linda searched her mind for topics of conversation, but she found none. And, unlike Mars, Klint made no effort to help her. If Klint hadn't been along, she would have run from the house in embarrassment. But Klint was here, and if she didn't want to appear an idiot in his eyes, she had to think of something to say.

"Virgie," Linda began, having decided to come right to the point, "I'm trying to help my uncle collect stories about your island, local-color stories that would enrich his book. I was hoping you'd be able to help me out."

A closed look came over Virgie's face. Her smile vanished, and even her voice dulled to a monotone.

"I be no storyteller, Miss Linda. I just cook. That my business. I be no storyteller."

There was a finality about Virgie's words that told Linda that further pleading would get her nowhere. In the silence that followed, Linda heard a tree branch scrape against a window screen and wished she could disappear. When Virgie left the table to perform some kitchen errand, Linda whispered to Klint:

"I blew it! What did I do wrong? She clammed up completely."

Klint shrugged. "You did nothing wrong. I'll see what I can do when she comes back."

"I'm afraid to even mention a turtle voyage," Linda said. "I could ruin Uncle Sheldon's chances if I said the wrong thing."

Klint nodded, and when Virgie returned to the table, he changed the subject.

"Virgie, surely you haven't been working in the garden wearing that beautiful ring?"

He nodded at the gold band set with a ruby-red stone that Virgie wore on her right forefinger.

"You know I never take ring off," Virgie said. "It be on finger since long before you born."

"It was part of Blackbeard's loot, wasn't it?"

"Huh!" Virgie snorted. "You know better! You try make me look bad in front of company? Blackbeard a no-good pirate. The ring once belong to Sir Henry Morgan, a servant of the king."

"I'm not trying to make you look bad," Klint laughed. "I'm just trying to get you to tell Linda about yourself. *You're* local color, Virgie. At least to the mainlanders, you are. Few people have had the interesting experiences you've had. Tell Linda about your ring."

The closed look disappeared from Virgie's face, and she beamed first at Klint and then at Linda.

"Why not you say to tell you about de ring? It be no secret. It be handed down in my family from Sir Henry Morgan. He was a privateer for England's king hundreds of years ago, when England warred with Spain."

"But when the war ended, Sir Henry

kept right on looting," Klint said. "Then he was just an ordinary pirate. And he used this island for a hangout. That's when he met your many-greated grandmother and led her astray like the villain he was."

"He may not married her like today with a preacher man and all, but my many-greated grandmother, she be married to Sir Henry in her own way. This be her wedding ring. Sir Henry no villain. Even the king make him governor of Jamaica."

"Lieutenant-governor," Klint corrected with a twinkle in his eye. "I'll have to admit that Morgan settled down. He hated the thought of a rope around his neck. There's probably still a seaful of loot from his escapades lying right off the shores of Grand Cayman."

"Really, Klint?" Linda said, for a moment forgetting her shyness of Virgie.

"Don't you be getting no ideas, Miss Linda," Virgie said. "Sir Henry's ghost guards any treasure that be on that ocean floor. He guards. Nobody make him give it up."

"You really believe that ghost story, don't you, Virgie?" Klint asked.

Virgie sat up straight and took a sip of water before replying, "Of course I believe."

"Have you ever seen it?" Klint asked.

Virgie shook her head. "My great-granddaddy saw it. He tole me when I be a little girl. I don't go looking for ghost. But I know it there. It protects its own."

Now that Virgie was talking freely, Klint brought up the subject of a turtle hunt. "Do you suppose Captain Taurus would make another turtle voyage for the benefit of a writer?"

"The captain be purely mule-stubborn," Virgie said. "But for you I might mention it to him."

Klint had made his point and didn't belabor it. Instead, he rose, thanked Virgie for a wonderful meal just as if she had prepared it, and ushered Linda outside to their bicycles.

When they were out of sight of Virgie's home, Linda could contain her feelings no longer. "I really made a mess of that. Virgie wouldn't have warmed up to me at all if you hadn't been there to say the right things. I'm not going to be any good to Uncle Sheldon. He should have brought someone else with him."

"You have to be interested in people before you can talk to them," Klint said. "You went to Virgie thinking only of your uncle and how scared you were. But don't feel bad about it. You'll learn with practice. And you'll have to learn. I was just giving you a lesson today. Next time you may be on your own."

"Then I'll flop," Linda said. "I'll never get anyone to talk to me."

Klint stopped his bicycle in the shade of a palmetto, and when Linda drew up beside him, he leaned over and kissed her.

"I'll talk to you. I think you're very special."

"Everyone is very special to you," Linda said, looking deep into his eyes. "Virgie. Uncle Sheldon. Kimo in the turtle crawl. Everyone. You're a miracle worker."

"Miracles are homemade. You'll come up with one before you leave here. But I hope you won't get discouraged and leave too soon. You're like a closed book, and I want to know you better."

Linda's relaxed, easy feeling about Klint vanished. She felt suddenly as if he were analyzing her, trying to figure her out as he would a puzzle. She thought longingly of Mars. Mars was always so preoccupied with himself and his own big ideas that she had never felt he thought about her deeply. In a way that had been nice. She didn't want to be an open book to anyone.

Chapter Five

The days came and went like the endless waves that swept onto the shore and then disappeared. There was a sameness about them, yet they were all different in detail. Sometimes Linda even forgot that she was on trial, and she could hardly believe it when the calendar told her that June had arrived.

Where had the month gone? She had thought she might be bored with nothing more to do than dispense a few pills and plan ulcer-diet menus, but this had not been the case. Those had been minor duties, yet they were important; they were details that Uncle Sheldon would have ignored had he been alone.

Linda's major duty lay, as Dr. Mercer had predicted, in keeping her uncle in an optimistic frame of mind. She soon noticed that mornings were danger times, and she learned to keep some good news on hand to cheer him out of his low moods. As yet she had been unable to force herself to approach strangers, to build warm relationships that resulted in the spontaneous outpourings that could be used as grist for a literary mill. But with Klint's help Linda did get around the island. Although she failed to supply stories, at least she pointed her uncle to where the action was.

Linda tried to suggest a new place for her uncle to visit each morning that his mood was low. Getting him out of his room and away from the lodge usually improved his mental outlook. Later he would return to his typewriter with his mind overflowing with ideas.

Uncle Sheldon worked most efficiently in the afternoons, and he was as glad to have Linda leave him alone as she was to be on her own. Their schedule suited Klint, too. Linda had lost count of the times he had taken her swimming or sailing or diving. Klint had become a part of her life that she would miss when this half year ended.

She knew she depended on Klint too much. She was the sort of person who didn't need a lot of people around — just one or two trusted friends were enough. Or at least she tried to tell herself that this was true; it removed the necessity for putting herself out to meet new people. Usually Klint was glad enough to be alone with her, but one June day he appeared at her door with a new idea.

"Are you free for the afternoon?" he asked, hands thrust deep into the pockets of his khakis.

Linda nodded. "Uncle Sheldon's going to be busy organizing material on pirate caches and on Pedro's Castle, where Henry Morgan was supposed to have lived. We climbed that dank staircase to see his former quarters this morning. It's a fascinating place."

"A villain named Pedro 'the Terrible' Gomez is supposed to have forced slaves who were stolen from Jamaica to build the castle for him," Klint said. "Morgan took over later. It's quite a tourist attraction. But I get weary of pirates and treasures. Would you like to watch some islanders engaged in the practical art of rope making?"

"Sounds great. What kind of rope?"

"They make lines that are used on the turtle schooners, or anywhere else where high-quality rope is needed. Captain

Taurus says that our Cayman thatch rope is better than any sisal or hemp cordage he's ever used. I'll take you to where the islanders are making the rope, but I can't stay with you. I have to come back and help Dad paint a cottage. We'll have to bicycle. Think it's too hot?"

"I can always cool off with a dip in the sea," Linda said. "Surely there'll be a story in this rope making that will interest Uncle Sheldon. But I hate talking to strangers. Can't we wait until someday when you can stay?"

"Want to invite your uncle to go along?"

Linda shook her head. "He's busy and happy. Maybe I can take him to visit the rope factory some morning when he's in a down mood." Linda did want Uncle Sheldon to go, but she knew she mustn't ask. They had had a strenuous morning of sightseeing. If her uncle became overly tired, he might become depressed and ill. And too much physical activity always aggravated his cough.

"It isn't exactly a factory," Klint said. "Don't get me wrong. I just happened to see Leo King at the Lighthouse last night, and he mentioned that he was working rope this afternoon. They're braiding it. That's a special process, not one you'll see every day."

Linda was silent for a moment. The Lighthouse was one of the few night spots on the island, and she wondered who Klint had taken there. But that was none of her business. None at all. She tried to squelch the unheralded twinge of jealousy that nagged at her.

"Is Leo King a good friend of yours?" she asked.

"As good as any," Klint said. "There are only a few thousand people on all three islands, so we're all fairly well acquainted. Everyone knows Leo. He's a good turtler." Klint headed toward the bicycle-rental stall, and Linda fell into step at his side.

"If he's so good, why isn't he out with Captain Taurus?"

"He was supposed to be, but Taurus sailed without him because Leo was drunk when it was time for the crew to board ship. Taurus allows no drinking on the *Tortuga*, and he's stubborn enough to enforce his rules even when it means leaving a good man behind. My guess is that Leo will be sober next time. He's missed out on earning a lot of money. There's not much cash in rope."

"Maybe Leo's just as stubborn as Captain Taurus," Linda mused.

"No chance." Klint pedaled into the

breeze. "Virgie's the only person on Grand Cayman who really stands up to the captain. Must be her pirate blood."

Linda wished she could back out of this trip. When Klint had asked her if she was busy, she had thought they would be doing something together. After a few minutes of pedaling in the humid air, perspiration began to bead on her forehead and upper lip, and her cotton blouse felt as if it had been pasted to her back. She was about to beg for a rest when Klint spoke.

"There it is, up ahead. In that shed."

"I hate to barge in on a bunch of men, Klint. It just doesn't look right."

"Oh, there'll be some women there, too. I wouldn't take you anywhere that was improper for you to go."

They rode toward the open shed, but instead of stopping when they reached it, Linda rode on past.

"What's the idea?" Klint asked. "You expect them to come out and introduce themselves?"

"Maybe they're too busy to bother with sightseers," Linda said.

"They've got forever to finish that rope," Klint assured her. "Come on, I'll introduce you. But then you're on your own. It'll be a good experience for you. Besides, I've got to get back to the lodge. Pretend you're your Uncle Sheldon. Ask yourself how he would go about getting a story from the men."

Linda wanted nothing more than to play her vanishing-cream game, to go back to her cottage and forget all about rope making. She could tell her uncle where the men were working, and he could come and see the process for himself. But that wasn't true. She couldn't use this jaunt to pull her uncle from a dreary mood unless she were enthusiastic about the subject. And she couldn't be enthusiastic unless she really knew about it.

Following Klint's lead, Linda turned her bicycle around and rode back to the shed.

"Leo," Klint called, "come meet a friend of mine."

A tall man with a mane of hair sweeping back from his face walked toward them. His faded dungarees fitted him like a second skin, and he moved with the graceful glide of a cat. His eyes demanded Linda's attention.

"Leo, this is Linda Carrol from the lodge. She's helping her uncle write a book, and she'd like to know more about your rope business. May she spend some time here watching and learning?"

"She be welcome." Leo grinned at Linda, showing white teeth in a crescent curve of mouth. "I'll take good care of her."

"See you later, Linda. Leo won't mind if you take notes."

Klint waved a farewell and rode away, and Linda fumbled in her handbag on the pretext of finding a notebook and a pencil. She felt Leo King's eyes on her, and she wanted to run like a rabbit. But pride held her to the spot. When she at last had the paper and pencil in hand, she looked up at Leo.

"I understand you're braiding today," she said.

"Right," Leo replied.

"I've always wanted to see how it's done."

"You're welcome to watch." He led the way to where he and another man had been working on long strands of rope. "Make yourself comfortable."

With those words Leo turned his attention to his co-worker, and Linda relaxed. Clearly, she was on her own. And just as clearly she had somehow missed an opportunity to learn the fundamentals of Caymanian rope making. Leo had been friendly enough, but just watching wasn't good enough. Linda needed an explanation of what she was seeing.

In one area a woman clad in a starched housedress was splitting dry leaves into strips, and another woman was twisting the strips into strands. Linda smiled and the women smiled back, but she didn't know how to approach them.

"Where do these leaves come from?" Linda asked at last.

The first woman giggled. "From trees. The thatch, she grows wild. We gather the leaves and dry them. We split them and twist them."

Linda thanked the woman and wrote down what she had said. She couldn't force herself to approach Leo King again, so after a short while she waved good-bye to the woman who had talked to her and mounted her bicycle.

She hadn't ridden far when she met Klint headed in her direction. When he drew near, she could see his smile.

"Didn't have to paint after all. Someone mixed the wrong color into the paint. Mom's fit to be tied. Now Dad has to re-order and wait for the stuff to arrive. Seen all the rope making you're interested in?"

"Klint, I just couldn't talk! I'd ask a question and they'd just sort of close up.

Your friend Leo told me I could watch, but just watching isn't enough."

"Come on, we'll go back. I'll help you get enough information to spark your uncle's interest."

Klint kept his promise. Where Linda had been unable to get any information, Klint received detailed replies to all his questions. And all he did was to ask Leo why his rope was better than other ropes.

Linda learned that considerable skill was required to insert the end of a new strip into the forming rope at the right time. She learned that it took additional skill to twist it hard enough so that the pieces didn't slip apart. Leo showed her how the ends of the strands were attached to spindles, which were rotated in opposite directions by two people at each end. At Klint's request he showed them how a cob, a piece of wood with three grooves in it, was slid along the rope as it was twisted to prevent it from knotting.

When Linda and Klint left the ropemakers, Linda had solid factual material to present to her uncle.

"You were great, Klint. I could never have gotten all this information alone."

"You have to learn to ask the right questions," Klint said. "If you penetrate right to the core of another person's interest, you'll usually get what you're after. Leo's interested in making good rope, so when I asked him why his was better than others, he was willing to talk freely. Most people are overjoyed when someone shows honest interest in their work, and they'll usually try to reward that interest."

Linda and Klint stopped along the shore to cool themselves with a wade into the surf. When they finally arrived back at the Pirates' Rendezvous, barefooted and disheveled, Linda had a surprise in store for her. Mars Ramsey was waiting outside her cottage. Dressed in gray slacks and a yellow silk shirt, Mars looked as if he had just stepped out of a fashion advertisement.

"Mars! Whatever are you doing here?" Linda gasped.

Without bothering to answer, Mars threw his arms around her and kissed her soundly. Linda felt her face grow hot clear to the roots of her hair. When Mars released her, she turned to Klint.

"Klint, I'd like you to meet Mars Ramsey. He's an old friend of mine from Miami."

"I thought perhaps the two of you had met before," Klint said, smiling as he shook Mars's hand.

"Klint, you've heard me speak of Mars. Why didn't you tell me he had written for reservations?"

"Because he didn't," Klint replied.

Linda looked at Mars. "You mean you came without —"

"Those reservation rules are for other people." Mars grinned. "This is the off season. I knew there'd be room for me somewhere. Where's your uncle? Why don't I tell all of you about my plans over a seafood dinner?" Mars's lavish gesture made it clear that he included Klint in his invitation.

"Sorry, but no, thanks," Klint said. "I work at the desk during the dinner hour." He smiled at Linda, and as he walked away Linda knew he wasn't the least bit jealous of Mars. There was no animosity in the air. It was as if Mars had simply come to claim a long-lost possession and Klint was totally engrossed in analyzing the unexpected owner.

Linda invited Mars to have a chair on the porch while she changed for dinner. Up until now she had been too surprised at seeing him to realize how she felt. She was overjoyed. And when Uncle Sheldon informed her that he was dining with the

McKlintocks, she was happy. Now she and Mars could dine alone. It would be like old times. She put on the blue sheath and bubble earrings that Mars especially liked.

"How did you get time off to come all this way to see me?" she asked him when they were seated in the dining hall.

"My plans with Acme Chemical didn't work out as I had hoped," Mars told her. "So I thought I'd see what sort of things were going on on Grand Cayman. I've joined the bug boys. They'll be here almost as long as you will."

Linda paused until the waitress finished setting a lobster dinner before her.

"I called our order in ahead," Mars said. "Okay?"

Linda nodded, wondering what would have happened if it hadn't been all right. "The bug boys? Who on earth are they?"

"The entomology crew that's here to figure out a solution to the mosquito problem. I've signed on as their secretary."

"Secretary! Mars, you can't mean it. Why would a person with your ambition and education settle for a job as a secretary?"

"To be near you, of course," Mars replied. "What's more important than that?"

Linda was speechless. She was also flattered. As usual Mars was sweeping her off her feet. "I can't let you do this, Mars. You shouldn't lose five months' time fooling around here when you could be advancing yourself in a big company somewhere."

"Maybe entomology will be my line," Mars said, sipping his coffee. "I'm not wasting time. I had a purpose in mind years ago when I learned shorthand and typing. Secretaries learn *who* as well as *how,* and *who* is always more important. In this world it's not what you know, but who you know."

"I always pictured secretaries as girls who had taken dead-end jobs to occupy their time until they were ready to get married," Linda said.

"Maybe some girls do," Mars agreed. "But your smart women's libbers will start as secretaries and chew their way to the top of their organization. And I'm all for equal rights. That's why I'm starting out as a secretary for the bug boys. Alexander Hamilton. Billy Rose. Irwin S. Cobb. They all started out as secretaries. If it was good enough for them, it's good enough for me. What are you doing tonight, Blondie?"

"Whatever you say," Linda replied. "Uncle Sheldon usually retires early. As soon as I've given him his evening medication, I'm free."

"How about a stroll along the beach? I've always wanted to propose to a girl on a moonlit beach on Grand Cayman Island."

"Always?"

"Always. Say, how's your job going?"

"Not so great." Linda told Mars of her duties and her misgivings about them, yet she couldn't bear to tell him that this seemingly simple job could make or break her nursing career.

"Uncle Sheldon's really counting on me, Mars. And so is Dr. Mercer. Uncle Sheldon's health is so tied up with his work that it frightens me. If I fail him, Dr. Mercer will lose professional respect for me, and I'll have lost all confidence in myself."

Suddenly Linda was aware that Mars wasn't paying attention. He had tuned her out. Was she really invisible?

Chapter Six

To Linda's great surprise, Mars seemed seriously interested in the work of the entomology crew. He reported for work each morning and accompanied the men into the swampy areas or wherever else their work took them. He was free in the evenings, and Linda saw him almost every night unless Uncle Sheldon needed her.

If Klint objected to Mars's presence, he kept it to himself. Whenever he wasn't working, he spent his afternoons with Linda. And Linda was becoming more and more confused. Although Mars knew she wasn't ready for marriage, he repeated his airy proposal every day. Mars was fun to be with. He charmed her with his smiles and his lavish attention. On the other hand, Klint was sparing with his compliments and tended to analyze, to offer advice — advice designed to shape up the weaknesses in Linda's personality. But he never belabored his points, and Linda knew that Klint wouldn't bother to try to help her if he didn't think her someone special. It was rather pleasant to be a special person for Klint McKlintock.

One Sunday in mid-June Linda burst into the cottage with the news that the McKlintocks would take all the guests for a sail on the *Hawksbill.* She could hardly believe it when Uncle Sheldon refused to go along.

"I'm not wasting a whole day away from my typewriter when I can stay right here and work." Uncle Sheldon contemplated the toe protruding through his sneaker.

"The sail will give you a new perspective on island life," Linda said. "Even the entomology crew is taking time off for the trip."

"I'm not going." He flopped down at his desk and rolled a sheet of paper into his typewriter. "I'd get seasick, and I'm sure that salt air would make my cough worse."

"But you plan to go on a turtle voyage," Linda reminded him. "How will you cope then?"

"That's different." He scowled and began typing, his moonlike face dark with gloom.

"All right," Linda sighed. "If that's the

way you want it. But this may be your only chance to travel on a schooner under sail. Captain Gibraltar's *Tortuga* has diesel engines now, I understand. I don't suppose it would be hard for you to imagine how life really used to be on a turtle voyage under sails. I know *I* could never do it, but I suppose it doesn't really matter. All that has passed from the present-day scene."

As she prepared his medicine for him, she watched him out of the corner of her eye to catch his reaction to her sly barb. He ripped the paper from the machine, wadded it up, and plunked it into the wastebasket.

"That's the trouble with you young people," Uncle Sheldon snorted. "No imagination. You'd take a schooner sail like the one planned today with no thought for the past. None whatsoever. Why, the sailors that ploughed these seas under canvas had more nautical knowledge in their little toes than the fancy skippers of modern yachts have in their heads. Where's my straw hat? What did I do with my sunglasses?"

Linda squelched a smile as she handed her uncle his battered hat and his glasses. She didn't fuss about his ragged shoes or his frayed shirt. She had won her point.

The shine of eager anticipation had replaced the dismal gloom on his face. Dr. Mercer would have been proud of her.

A few minutes later they stepped onto the dock, and Linda felt the sway of the heavy timbers as the water surged beneath them. The smell of the ocean and the taste of salt spray made a sensory foil for the sleek lines of the *Hawksbill*, its white sails billowing against the bright blue sky. Klint shouted orders to a small crew of Caymanians, some of whom Linda recognized.

Kimo, whom she had seen in the turtle crawl, was bare to the waist, his muscled shoulders gleaming in the sunlight. He wore a grimy pair of patched trousers and a pair of sneakers that made Uncle Sheldon's look new. The two men she had seen in the catboat were there, too. Neither of them wore shirts, but their trousers were faded but clean blue denim. At first Linda hardly recognized Leo King under a felt sombrero with a leather chin strap, but Klint reintroduced them.

The McKlintocks made the passengers comfortable, arranging and rearranging canvas deck chairs and cushions. Klint looked the part of a captain in a khaki shirt and pants and a visor hat, but there was so much confusion aboard that Linda doubted that the schooner would ever leave the dock.

After reserving a deck chair for herself and one for her uncle, Linda explored the schooner. The *Hawksbill* was about seventy feet long and perhaps twenty feet across. Heavy masts rose from the deck, and fore and aft sails snapped in the wind. At the widest part of the deck two catboats rested on their sides, and between them Virgie and Gem worked in a makeshift galley.

"Guess we're having lunch aboard," Linda said to her uncle.

"I brought some crackers along just in case." He reached into his pocket and offered Linda a saltine, which she refused.

"Have you seen belowdecks?" Mars asked, joining Linda and her uncle.

"Mars!" Linda drank in Mars's brass-buttoned blazer and white slacks that made him look more like the ship's captain than Klint. "That's a neat outfit!"

"Just some old rags I happened to find in the back of my closet." Mars grinned. "This schooner's a fairly authentic replica of the old turtlers, did you know?" He nodded to a ladder leading below the main deck. "That's the hold where the big greens were stored. The crew's fo'c'sle's down there, too — where the crew sleeps."

Mars took a childlike delight in showing Linda more of the schooner, and she enjoyed his company, but she was ready to sit down with her uncle and rest when Klint ordered his crew to weigh anchor. In a few moments the sails caught the wind, and the *Hawksbill* left land behind them.

Casuarina trees leaned away from the wind, and frigate birds wheeled in the sky. At first they skimmed over smooth seas in the lee of the island, then Klint beat a course toward the white-capped depths. For a few seconds the water spread thin and the keel churned sand. Klint jumped onto the rail at the bow to guide them clear of the shallows. The sun shafted down like a spotlight and made the water seem pale. But at last they broke through a smother of white breakers into cobalt-blue waves.

While the *Hawksbill* circled Grand Cayman, Uncle Sheldon observed and took notes. Linda was content to sit at his side, but Mars grew restless and paced the deck. After he had been gone for some time, Klint stopped by to speak to Linda. He had removed his hat, and the sun cast reddish glints into his sandy hair. He had never looked so handsome.

"Want to see some flying fish?" he asked.

"On board?" Linda searched the deck with her eyes.

"Come to the bow." Klint offered his arm for support. "They may jump aboard, but right now they're playing in the spray up ahead."

Linda smiled at the calypso lilt in Klint's voice as they walked to the bow. With her hand still on his arm for support, she peered over the rail into the sea.

"There!" She pointed. "I see one. There! By that patch of seaweed." She watched a fish on translucent wings sail free of the bow wave and skid away, then she looked up at Klint. "It's a wonderful schooner. You must be terribly proud of it."

Klint stared dreamily out at the sea. "I've sold her. Just yesterday. That's why we organized the sail for today."

"Klint! How could you! All that work!"

"I made a good profit," he said. "Don't worry about that. I'm out of debt now, and I'll build another schooner with my own capital soon."

"Will it be like the *Hawksbill*?"

Klint nodded. "This is a Cayman schooner. It's similar to the North Atlantic fishing ships of the eighteen hundreds. The hull design came from Nova Scotia. It may be old-fashioned, but it serves its purpose. And it gives the Pirates' Rendezvous lots of local color. Last winter's guests loved it." His eyes were still on the sea.

"What are you thinking?" Linda asked.

"I'm thinking that I'd like to start my own schooner service between the Caymans and Florida. I think I told you that. It's been my dream ever since I was a kid. Guess my tutor planted the idea in my mind. He came here each year by plane. And how that man hated to fly! We finally arranged for him to travel by cargo boat."

"Would you pilot the boat yourself?"

"I'd have to study some navigation, but I'm sure I could do it. No sails, of course. I would have to make it practical enough to realize a profit. The idea's been tried before, and it failed, but the Caymans weren't well known then. Each year more and more tourists come here. The tourist trade is good for everyone. I want to do my part to build it up."

Klint stopped talking abruptly, and Linda knew that he had revealed more of his inner thoughts and desires than he had intended. She smiled to herself. She felt that she knew him better than she had an hour ago. Klint was a man with a dream, a dream he had held from childhood. He knew exactly where he wanted to go, what he wanted to do, and slowly but surely he was working to make his dream come true.

"Hey! There you are!" Mars hurried toward them, his head thrust forward and his arms swinging free. At first Linda thought he was talking to her, but then she realized that his eyes were on Klint.

"Troubles?" Klint said, his voice calm and sure.

"None." Mars grinned. "I just want some information. I heard some of the crew talking about diving for black coral. Do you really have that stuff around here?"

Klint smiled and looked at a spot just above Mars's head. "Sorry, you'll have to excuse me right now. I want to bring us in nearer to land."

Klint walked off, and Linda led Mars back to the deck chairs.

"Mr. Burr, what do you know about black coral?" Mars asked. "I heard some crewmen whispering about it a while ago. They stopped talking when I joined them. Is there some big secret about it?"

Uncle Sheldon shrugged. "If there's a secret I want in on it. When I finish this book, the Caymans should hold few secrets from the world. But I've never heard anything about black coral. I know they dive for it in the waters around Hawaii. It's quite rare, from what I'm told."

Before they could pursue the subject further, Mrs. and Mr. McKlintock announced that lunch was ready.

"Virgie and Gem will serve cafeteria-style," Mrs. McKlintock said. "The menu consists of clam chowder and watercress sandwiches, coffee or tea. You may eat in your deck chairs or wherever you'll be comfortable."

Mars needed no urging. He maneuvered Linda and her uncle to the head of the line. Once he saw that their position was good, he returned to the subject of the coral.

"It's used for jewelry and ornaments," Mars said. "Could be there's a whole new industry here just waiting to be developed by a sharp operator like yours truly."

Suddenly Klint appeared at their side, his face masked with an expression Linda couldn't read.

"How about changing the subject?" Klint's eyes bored into Mars's. "I'll explain later."

He strode off, leaving Mars looking surprised. Then Mars became angry, and a red flush washed over his face.

"That guy's not going to tell me what to

talk about! Who does he think he is, anyway!"

"Mars, people are staring," Linda admonished.

"Let them stare. Who cares! I want to know about —"

Linda nudged Mars none too gently. "Klint said he'd explain later. Give him a chance. Don't cause a scene."

Mars clamped his jaws together and didn't open them again until they were seated and ready to eat. True to his word, Klint joined them. He declined Linda's invitation to sit down, and she wondered if he preferred towering over them in order to give himself more of an aura of authority.

"I didn't mean to be rude," Klint said, looking directly at Mars. "But Virgie's husband died in a quest for black coral. You were at the head of the line where she could overhear your words. I was merely trying to spare her feelings."

"I thought your mother told us that her husband deserted her," Linda said.

"That's Virgie's story," Klint said, "and to her way of thinking, that's what happened. But most Caymanians read a different meaning into the facts."

"Give, boy, give," Uncle Sheldon said.

"Wait until I get my notebook. I sense a story here."

"You won't write anything that'll hurt Virgie?" Klint's eyes shone ice-blue.

"Nothing whatsoever," Uncle Sheldon promised. "I never flirt with lawsuits. That kind of stuff makes my publisher nervous."

"Virgie's husband was diving for black coral and he never returned." Klint shrugged. "It's as simple as that. The coral grows deep, and he had poor scuba equipment. His body was never found, but experts around here think that he dived too deep, stayed down too long, then surfaced too quickly and died of the bends."

"But his body," Linda said. "Wouldn't it wash ashore somewhere, sometime?"

"Perhaps. Perhaps not." Klint looked seaward. "Many sharks prowl these waters."

Linda shuddered. "But why would Virgie say her husband deserted her? I don't understand that at all."

"Remember the story she told us that day at her cottage? The one about the ghost who guards the pirate treasure?"

"Yes," Linda said.

"You may think that's just an interesting tale, but to Virgie that ghost is as real as you and Mars. There's no question in her mind that it exists. She warned her husband about the ghost, but he ignored her and went diving in what Virgie considered the danger area. Virgie feels that he deliberately deserted her by going there, that he deliberately walked into death. Black coral is a subject that we avoid in her presence."

"Ghosts! Bunk!" Mars pounded his chair arm so hard that he almost upset his chowder. "I don't believe in that kind of rot. Where are these coral beds? I'm going to have a look-see for myself."

"Where are they, Klint?" Linda asked.

For a long moment Klint was silent, and when he spoke he looked at Mars. "I'm not free to reveal the whereabouts of the coral beds. And you would be wise not to search them out." Without another word he turned and left them.

"What do you make of that?" Uncle Sheldon asked in amazement. "The boy's turned a mite unfriendly, I'd say. Maybe you can wheedle the info from him, Linda."

Linda felt a strange knotting in the pit of her stomach. How dare Klint act so secretive! It wasn't at all like him. And how dare Uncle Sheldon ask her to pry information from him! Surely even Dr. Mercer would consider such measures beyond the call of duty.

"Don't take it so hard, Linda," Mars said. "Let ole Klint keep his secrets. We can hunt for the coral without his help, can't we? I see divers all over the place around here."

"But you don't know where the black coral is," Linda protested. "There's a lot of water around here."

"We'll find out from Virgie," Mars said.

"You wouldn't!" Linda glared at him. "It wouldn't be fair to probe into old wounds. I'll have no part of that!"

"Who said anything about probing into old wounds? I won't even mention coral to her. But if she told you the pirate-ghost story, evidently she doesn't mind speaking of that. All we have to do is to find out where the ghost hangs out. Klint's already told us the rest. The so-called ghost was near the coral bed. You're not afraid, are you, Linda? You'll go with me to dive for the coral, won't you?"

"What about sharks?" Linda quavered. "And I can't dive very deep. I've never used scuba equipment, just a mask and snorkel."

"You don't have to dive," Uncle Sheldon

piped up, "but I want you to go along with Mars, and I'm inviting myself, too. Klint doesn't own these waters. If we stick with Mars, we may come up with a whole new chapter for my book."

Chapter Seven

Only because the thought of diving for black coral kept her uncle in high spirits did Linda agree to accompany him. His pleading tugged her in one direction, while Klint's veiled warning pulled her in another. But she reminded herself that she was a nurse. Nobody must influence her to do anything that was not in the best interest of her patient.

Linda forgot her differences with Klint the next morning when he appeared at her door, his face aglow. His eagerness was contagious, and even Uncle Sheldon smiled as he downed the capsules Linda had rationed out for him.

"The *Tortuga*'s in!" Klint wagged his head toward the north and jammed his hands into the pockets of his khakis. "If we hurry, you'll get to see the crew unload the turtles into the crawl. Come on! Dad's driving."

"Is there room?" Linda grabbed her sunglasses and scooped up a handful of sharpened pencils for her uncle.

"We'll crowd in somehow."

Klint led the way to the car, and when they reached it, they found Mars and part of the entomology crew already inside.

"Holiday?" Linda laughed.

"Guess the arrival of the *Tortuga* is always a holiday," Mars replied. "Hop in."

Linda counted eight people in the car as she wedged herself between her uncle and Mars. The air was unbearably hot as they drove along, and Linda felt moisture beading on her forehead and heard a mosquito singing at her ear.

The *Tortuga* lay heavy in the water, its crew swarming over the deck and in and out of the hold. The schooner had been painted a shade of green that almost matched the turquoise water.

"There's Captain Taurus," Linda said as they got out of the car.

"You've met him?" Mars mopped the sweat from his neck.

"No, but I'm sure that's he. The big one with the knobby hands and the legs like mango stumps. He's the only one aboard who looks like the Rock of Gibraltar."

"We cotch de turtle!" Captain Taurus

shouted to the McKlintocks when he saw them. "Come aboard and see de cotch."

"We'll watch from here," Klint shouted in reply. "We'll be in your way if we come aboard." He turned to Linda and her uncle. "Let's go downshore a way. We'll be able to see what's going on from there."

Mars tagged along, although he hadn't been included in the invitation. The sun beat down unmercifully as they watched the crew go to work unloading the turtles with the aid of a block and tackle. Each turtle was secured with a rope bridled to the base of its foreflippers. The men in the crawl released the animals from their ropes once they were submerged in the sea.

Linda counted fifty turtles before she lost interest. "Will they all fit into the crawl?"

"There are other crawls," Klint told her. "When this one is full, they'll go to another."

"Who buys all those creatures?" Linda asked.

"The Caymanians eat a lot of them, but many are slaughtered, and the meat is processed and shipped to foreign markets. A green turtle steak is a delicacy in the fancy restaurants in New York."

"I saw frozen turtle steaks at the airport," Linda said. "I guess tourists send them home as gifts. Hey look, Klint! Look at that one. It isn't green like the others."

"It's a hawksbill," Klint replied.

"Are they fit to eat?" Uncle Sheldon asked, his pencil skimming across a sheet of notepaper.

"That's a matter of opinion." Klint grinned. "I don't care to eat hawksbill. In fact, I think the myth that they're edible comes from Cayman Brac. There's a tortoise-shell industry there, and the natives have to talk up the product."

After many turtles had been released, Klint took Linda and her uncle to meet Captain Taurus. He had stepped ashore and was moving as if he couldn't adjust to the feel of solid land beneath his feet.

Linda could almost guess at the mental notes her uncle was taking, impressions that he would later transfer to paper. Captain Taurus was a beefy man, taller than most of his crew. His chest and shoulders were broad, his hair was dark, and his small ears looked almost out of place on so large a head. A lock of hair fell over his forehead, giving him a boyish look, but underlying all his physical attributes was his unwavering air of determination.

"Captain Taurus," Klint began, "I'd like

for you to meet a friend of mine, Miss Linda Carrol. She's staying at the lodge with her uncle, who is an author."

Linda offered her hand, and the captain shook it in a crunching grasp that almost made her cry out.

"Pleased to meet with you, ma'am." The captain's voice was deep and throaty as he regarded Linda with sea-faded eyes.

"It must be good to be home again," Linda commented, not knowing what one should say to a sea captain.

"Good, mahn, good." Captain Taurus grinned. "De best." Then he turned and bellowed an order at one of his crewmen. The man dashed away and returned presently with a pink flowerpot bearing an orchid plant glowing with lavender blossoms.

Captain Taurus took the plant and presented it to Linda. "When I sail de Caribbean, I take a bit of land with me. For luck. Now I need it no more. It is yours."

"Why, thank you!" Linda exclaimed. "I'll take good care of it for you."

"Yours to keep," Captain Taurus said. "No need for a plant until next voyage — next year."

Linda eased into the background as other islanders came forward to welcome the captain. Mars had disappeared, and

Linda stayed close to her uncle, trying to shield him from the buffeting of the crowd.

"I didn't like what he said about not going out again until next year," Uncle Sheldon said.

"That's probably his usual routine," Linda said. "He has no way of knowing that you want to go on a voyage. And if I were you, I wouldn't mention it to him too soon."

"Why not? He might as well know so he can plan accordingly."

"Wait," Linda pleaded. "Look at him, Uncle Sheldon. Look how he stands. He's dug his heels in, folded his arms, and stuck out his chin. That man's happy to be home, and you're not likely to persuade him to leave again very soon." Linda looked at the pot of orchids in her hand and laughed. "I always thought sailors were tough men who loved the sea, but I'll bet Captain Taurus gets homesick before he's out of sight of land. Whoever heard of a sea captain raising orchids aboard ship!"

"I'd bring you orchids every day if only you'd let me," Mars said, coming up to them in time to hear the tag end of Linda's words. "I may not have orchids, but I do have news — for both of you."

"I can wait to hear mine," Uncle

Sheldon said dryly. "I want to mingle with these people — get the feel of the crowd, the sound of the welcome."

"Don't forget to catch the stench of the hold," Mars gibed.

Uncle Sheldon nodded. "It all adds up to a picture of the Caymans that my readers will appreciate."

"What is it, Mars?" Linda asked as her uncle elbowed his way into the crowd.

"Virgie blabbed," Mars said with a look of triumph. "Oh, she doesn't know she blabbed, but she did. I believe she was feeling a bit out of it, what with Captain Taurus getting all the attention. It was no trouble at all to get her to talk about her pirate ghost. It seems that a coral reef completely surrounds Grand Cayman, but this special ghost haunts an area about ten miles from here and straight out to sea. Will you go diving with me tomorrow, Linda?"

"Don't you have to work?" Linda asked.

"I'll beg a day off," Mars told her. "I've been steady on the job ever since I got here. There must be some fringe benefits, like a half day free for diving."

Linda hesitated, then she told Mars the truth. "I have an appointment with Klint for tomorrow, Mars. We'll have to make it another day."

"Klint! Klint!" Mars exploded. "I don't care if you pass the time with that creep when I'm not around, but when I'm on hand, you're my girl, see?"

"Klint's going to take me to Cayman Brac and maybe on to Little Cayman. I'm really taking the trip to help Uncle Sheldon. I can find the spots he'll be interested in, then he can fly over later and go right to them. It'll save him a lot of running around."

"I don't like it. I'll take you island hopping, if that's what you want. But tomorrow we dive."

"No, Mars." Linda kept her voice firm. "Really, you aren't ready yet. You have to find a diving buddy. I can't dive deep, and you'll need a partner for safety's sake."

"I suppose you're right. But you save the day after tomorrow for me, all right? We'll go out to the Cayman trench and dive until we find the black coral."

"Cayman trench?" Linda repeated. "What's that?"

"The water between the Caymans and southeast Cuba is mostly shallow," Mars said. "But there's a marine chasm out there that drops off to a depth of four miles or more. That's the spot we're hunting. Virgie says that all the easy treasure in shallow waters has been found, but loot that sank into the trench is still there. I didn't tell her that our treasure was black coral."

"Let's hike back to the lodge, Mars," Linda suggested. "The wind's changed, and the stench from that turtler is blowing right at us. I'll go tell Uncle Sheldon. He can stay and come back later in the McKlintocks' car."

Linda performed her errand, and when they were on their way toward the lodge, she began to question Mars about the coral.

"If that stuff grows so deep in the sea, you'll never be able to see it without artificial light."

"Wrong," Mars said. "These Cayman sands are so white they reflect the light. I've been quizzing other divers. They say the water is as clear as rum even below a two-hundred-foot depth."

"Your enthusiasm is catching. I'm almost as eager to go diving as you are."

"I'll rent a boat, and I'll get Virgie to pack us a lunch. Of course, I'll want your uncle to go along. The information and the coral we bring back will be unique. But better not say anything to Klint. I have a feeling he'd go out of his way to jinx our plans."

Chapter Eight

Although the uproar over the *Tortuga*'s return diminished somewhat by evening, Linda's personal feelings rose on a crescendo of excitement. The thought of diving for black coral made the hairs along the back of her neck tingle, even though she knew it would be Mars and not she herself who would descend to the great depths. And the thought of her visit to Cayman Brac with Klint kept her awake for most of the night. But the next morning she felt more rested than she thought possible.

Uncle Sheldon awakened in a good mood, and Linda sensed that it was her own exuberance that buoyed his spirits. How lucky she was that neither the diving venture nor the trip to Cayman Brac would require her to face strangers.

"Write it down," Uncle Sheldon said over and over, his round eyes imploring.

"Whatever strikes eye, ear, nose, or tongue, write it down. If you don't you'll forget something important. Drat this bronchitis, anyway! If Doc Mercer's remedies were half as good as he claims them to be, I'd be flying over with you this morning."

"It'll still be there later," Linda said as she grabbed the white straw purse that matched her shoes. "But don't worry, I'll write everything down."

When Klint arrived, he was his usual calm self, and his demeanor was a thermostat that controlled Linda's excitement.

Mr. McKlintock drove them to the sleepy village of Georgetown and on to the airport, where he waited until he saw them board an interisland plane. The craft seemed small compared to the plane that brought Linda to Grand Cayman from Miami, and although she wasn't frightened, she was glad that Klint was with her.

Their takeoff was smooth, but it seemed to Linda that she had hardly unfastened her seat belt when it was time to refasten it for landing. The touchdown was bumpy, and she clung to Klint's arm and closed her eyes.

The airport in Cayman Brac was much smaller than the one at Georgetown, but Klint managed to rent a rusty-looking jeep for the day. They drove off down a crooked sandy road with the sun beating on their heads and shoulders.

"Where are we going first?" Linda asked.

"I'll show you the ironshore," Klint said. "And take note of these dwarf coconut palms. Your uncle will probably be interested in them. The natives say that there used to be tall coconut palms here years ago, but they were killed off by disease and hurricanes. These are all that are left."

Linda made a note of that fact. "What's the ironshore?"

Klint slowed the jeep to avoid a hole in the road, and Linda felt road dust grit against her teeth.

"The ironshore's a flat, rigid plate that stretches along the edge of the island," Klint said. "Incidentally, this island isn't as big as Grand Cayman. It's only about twelve miles long and a couple of miles wide."

After they had driven a bit farther, Klint stopped the jeep and they got out. "We'll take a look around here for as long as you like, then we'll rent a boat and motor over to Little Cayman. It's just a spit and a fling from here. We'll eat lunch there."

Linda inhaled the dampness from the sea breeze as they walked toward an iron-gray beach. "Ironshore?" she said. "Does it get its name from the color?"

"From the color and from the sound. Listen." Pulling a knife from his pocket, Klint opened the blade and tapped on the plate of rock beneath their feet.

"It rings like metal!" Linda exclaimed, then spluttered as a spray of water drenched her from head to foot. "Where did that come from?"

Klint tried not to laugh. "Blowholes pock the ironshore in many places. The tide races in under this rigid plate we're standing on because the area is honeycombed with caves and niches. Sometimes the water is forced up through holes in the ironshore. Blowholes. That's what you just walked into. I should have warned you."

"Oh, well, we were going to swim after a while, weren't we?"

"That's what I like about you, Linda. You're a real sport."

Linda scribbled a few notes about the ironshore, and then they walked to the edge and peered over.

"There's a dropoff right here." Klint pulled her to his side. "Lean over and look down, and you'll see some of the caves I mentioned."

Linda saw a cave with multicolored tropical fish darting around its entrance. She shivered.

"I can believe all the pirate stories when I look at this. What better place could a villain find to hide his loot in? Have you ever explored any of these caves?"

"Lots of times when I was a kid. But I never found anything. All the easy spots have been searched again and again, and so have some of the not-so-easy ones. I don't want to rush you, but I want you to see this beach before we go to Little Cayman, and I'm already starving."

Linda followed Klint to the landward edge of sand where tumbled pieces of rock littered the ironshore.

"What's all this?" She picked up a rock the size of a baseball and kicked at another one shaped like a watermelon.

"It's coral," Klint replied. "It's been rounded and smoothed by the continual action of the water. We call them coral cobbles."

Linda looked at a surf-stacked ridge of cobbles nearly fifteen feet high. "I suppose the high tide flings them up here."

"Right. The word 'Brac' means cliff in Gaelic. This is literally the Cayman Cliff. The sea washes dead coral against the cliff and it stays here. Some of it breaks into cylinders or these bladelike shards you see."

After Linda had made all the notes she needed, they drove over an almost-deserted road to a small village where they could rent a boat. Linda found a place to change into her swimsuit, which she had in her straw bag. While she went to change, Klint went in search of sandwiches. When they met again on the beach, Klint led the way to a small boat with an outboard motor.

"I suppose this is safe," Linda said, trying not to sound scared. "There's an awful lot of sea out there."

"It's only a few miles to Little Cayman," Klint said. "I want you to have a picnic lunch on the most beautiful beach in the world."

Again Klint's manner calmed her, and she climbed into the boat and prepared to enjoy the trip. They cut through sun-splintered water, and in no time Linda saw the beach of Little Cayman. It was everything that Klint had promised. The white sand was deserted, and the cloudless blue sky looked down on only them. As Klint eased toward the shore he cut the motor and prepared to dive overboard.

"We have to swim in from here?" Linda asked.

"No. I'm just going to catch part of our lunch." Klint's tanned body disappeared under the surface, and in a few moments he came up at the stern. In one hand he clutched a huge pink conch. After heaving himself over the side of the boat, he steered closer to shore, and then they both splashed into the warm shallow water and pulled the boat up on the sand.

"I'm absolutely starved," Linda said.

"You'll love the conch," Klint promised.

"I'm starved, but I'll never eat raw shell-fish."

Klint shrugged and opened the bag of food he had purchased on Cayman Brac. Sitting in the shade of the boat, they enjoyed their sandwiches and milk. Then Klint broke open the conch, sliced the meat into small chunks, and poured over it a sauce that he took from the bag. When Linda declined to have the first taste, he began eating the conch with obvious relish.

"Oh, all right," Linda said. "I'll take just a small bite. Just a smidgen."

Klint gave her a bite, and she squinted her eyes. Then she opened them and looked at Klint. "That's delicious! What's in the sauce?"

"I've no idea. These island women keep

that sort of information a guarded secret. Virgie makes her own version on Grand Cayman, but I believe this is better."

"Better not let Virgie hear you say that," Linda laughed.

After they had eaten, they rested in the sand for several minutes. White gulls wheeled against the blue sky, screaming and crying but hardly moving their wings in flight. Miniature crabs skittered sideways across the packed sand, and Linda felt as if she and Klint were the only people on this small island.

"Little Cayman's entirely undeveloped," Klint said as if in response to Linda's thoughts. "Oh, there's a game club and one big mansion built by some millionaire, but that's all. That's why I wanted to bring you here."

"I don't understand."

"I wanted a very private place to ask you to marry me." Klint took Linda's hand and gazed into her eyes. "And I don't want an answer right this minute. I want you to think about it for as long as you need to. But you must know that I love you."

"I've often dreamed that you might," Linda said. "But in a setting like this, how does a girl tell a dream from the real thing?"

"I want you to know my plans." Klint

eased closer to Linda and put an arm about her shoulder. "I told you my dreams for a passenger line between the Caymans and Florida, but I also want to go into merchant shipping with headquarters in Miami. Of course, I'll be starting on a shoestring, but I know ships and I know the sea. I think I can make a success of a small shipping business."

"I'm no gold digger, you know," Linda said. "I'm not going to base my decision on how much money you plan to make."

"I didn't think you would. But you have a right to know what you'd be getting into. I want you to think it over. Carefully. For me marriage is a onetime thing. I don't want either of us to make a mistake."

How different Mars and Klint were! Linda sighed as they got back into the boat for the return trip to Cayman Brac. For all his personal secrecy, she felt that she knew Klint better than she had ever known anyone before. Of course, Mars's life was an open page, but the book was loose-leaf, and he kept changing the pages as he changed his mind about things.

Linda could hardly keep her mind on taking notes for her uncle the rest of the afternoon on Cayman Brac. They visited the village stores and a shop where craftsmen fashioned turtle shells into combs and brooches and clips.

It was not until they were on the flight back to Grand Cayman that Linda remembered her diving session with Mars the next day. Cautiously she mentioned it to Klint, and though he made no comment, she sensed a tenseness in him that had been absent before.

"Why not come with us, Klint?" she suggested. "Mars is going to rent a boat and hire someone to dive with him."

"He'll never do it," Klint replied. "Once the islanders find out that he's after black coral, they'll never help him. He'll discover that the boats are all rented and that no one knows how to dive that deep."

"But why? What's with the black coral, anyway?"

Klint looked out the window as he spoke. "Many of the islanders believe in that pirate ghost just as strongly as Virgie does. Mars Ramsey won't find one island boy brave enough to go diving with him into the trench."

Linda felt a coldness between herself and Klint. It was as if someone had thrust a plate glass between them. They could see each other, but they couldn't reach out to each other. Linda wondered if Klint's words were true. Would the island men refuse to dive with Mars because they were afraid of a ghost? Or would they refuse because they were afraid of Klint McKlintock? Linda wished she had followed Mars's advice and not mentioned the diving trip to Klint.

Chapter Nine

When they arrived back at the Pirates' Rendezvous, Linda was exhausted. She was glad that she had prepared her uncle's dinner menu before she left that morning, and she was just wishing she could fall into bed when Mars knocked on her door. He wore a cinnamon-colored shirt and slacks, and he seemed oblivious to the tropical heat.

"Come on, Blondie, I've made dinner reservations for two at the Surf Rider. Pull on your best threads and let's live."

"Oh, Mars!" Linda forced the dismay from her voice. "That sounds great, but I'll need time to freshen up. Can you give me an hour?"

"An hour! An hour away from you is like a day on a desert." Mars gestured dramatically. "But I'll survive if you'll be prompt."

"You have my word," Linda promised,

and went in to tell her uncle.

"Thought you were bone-tired," Uncle Sheldon said with a grin as he looked up from the notes Linda had given him.

"I was, but somehow Mars makes me forget it. I've got forever to rest. You don't mind my going out again, do you?"

"Of course not. I consider today's jaunt strictly business. I'll have to fly to Cayman Brac and check on some of these things."

"I'll leave your medicine and some water on a tray by your bed, and I want your promise that you'll take it."

"Never fear. Besides, I may be up when you return. I've some typing to do."

Linda closed the door between their rooms and stretched out on her bed for a short rest. Her mind flooded with questions. For all his lightheartedness, Mars had been begging her to marry him for months, and now Klint had entered her life in a big way. How was she going to cope?

She was not the kind to flirt, to play games, to keep men dangling needlessly. That was unfair. But she really didn't know her own mind. Could she manage a lifetime of being the dream girl Mars expected? He might faint if he saw her with Vicks on her throat or curlers in her hair.

And what about Klint? Could she heed

his gentle criticisms and grow to meet his standards? Life with Mars would never be boring, but on the other hand, marriage to Klint would be exotic and challenging. Linda tossed and squirmed until it was time to dress.

Mars arrived punctually, and in a borrowed car they drove over a white sand road to the Surf Rider. A jukebox wailed its cry into the night, and red and blue lights winked a neon welcome. As they stepped through the front door of the nightclub Linda saw Klint slip through the swinging doors that led to the kitchen. Had he seen her? Was he trying to avoid her? Linda could only make a guess.

"I called ahead with our order so we wouldn't have to wait," Mars said as a waitress ushered them to a secluded corner table. "Green turtle steak okay?"

Linda nodded, although she would rather have a salad.

"Are you all set to go diving with me tomorrow?" Mars asked.

Linda sighed. "You're still determined to find black coral?"

"Of course I am. Aren't you interested?"

"What Uncle Sheldon's interested in, I'm interested in," Linda said. "But I feel a premonition of danger."

"*Premonition!* Since when have you started feeling premonitions? Diving is diving. There's no sport with so many backup safety features."

"What about your equipment?"

"I knew before I came here that these islands were a diver's dream. I brought my own tank block and regulator assembly with me on the plane."

"You'll need a buddy," Linda reminded him. "You wouldn't dive alone, would you?"

"I would if there was no other way. But don't panic. Why do you think we came here tonight?"

"To eat," Linda said as the waitress set down their plates. The turtle steak gave off a delicious aroma all its own, and Linda realized she was hungrier than she had thought.

"To eat. Right. And to meet people who might dive with me. I understand that Captain Taurus hangs out here later in the evening. And Leo King's at that table near the kitchen. They'd both be good men to dive with, and they probably have access to a boat."

Linda looked at Leo, thinking that his white sport shirt made a perfect foil for his mane of dark hair. "Why not try a boat-rental service? I thought you were going to do that."

"Most of them are closed until the tourist season opens again. And I've met Taurus and Leo. I'd rather dive with someone I know."

Linda enjoyed her dinner and appreciated Mars's enthusiasm for the diving venture. But when he got ready to approach Leo, she became nervous. Mars sauntered to Leo's table as if he had nothing more important on his mind than mosquito eradication. They talked for a few minutes, then both returned to the table where Linda waited.

Linda nodded a greeting as Leo sat down across from her. A wisp of hair from the mane sweeping off his face kept falling over one eye, and his naturally slurred speech was heavy and coarse.

"I'll get right to the point," Mars said. "I'd like to hire you to dive with me tomorrow. In the trench. For black coral. Can we make a deal?"

Leo eased his position in the chair with the suppleness of a large cat. "Not me, mahn. Not me."

"But why not?" Mars asked. "I'll pay whatever the going rate happens to be. More fun than making rope all day."

"I be not interested." Leo shoved his chair back from the table, then leaned toward Mars and whispered, "Pirate ghost no like divers."

Leo glided back to his table, leaving Mars open-mouthed.

"Can you top that! I offer good money and he refuses. He must be putting me on. No grown man believes that ghost hokum."

Linda shrugged, knowing the uselessness of arguing. They lingered over coffee, danced to the blaring jukebox, and talked of diving and black coral. It was late when Captain Taurus Gibraltar entered the club. Before he had a chance to find a table, Mars approached him and offered him a seat at their table.

Captain Taurus placed his order, then settled down to listen to Mars. But when Mars finished talking, the captain's reaction was similar to Leo's.

"No, mahn, no. After the turtle voyage I be through with the sea for another year. No, mahn, no."

"You're not afraid of the pirate ghost that supposedly guards long-lost plunder, are you?"

"No, mahn, no. Me sister-in-law believes that yarn, but not me. I no dive because it be dangerous."

"More dangerous than a turtle hunt?" Mars looked his disbelief.

Captain Taurus nodded. "You listen, boy. You fool around with black coral, you end up dead of the bends. The bushes be two hundred feet or more straight down. You have to make the trip down and back in sixteen minutes."

"Who made up that rule?" Mars asked.

"Cayman divers who know their business," Captain Taurus replied. "You stay down too long, come up too quick, it's all over."

"But what about your ears?" Linda asked, surprised that she had the nerve to speak to the captain.

"That be one more problem. Diver must go down fast. Mos' any diver can go down two hundred feet if he has plenty time for stops to allow pressure to adjust."

"No amount of training or practice could make any difference in that respect," Mars said. "Either a guy can adjust to the pressure change or he can't."

"Right, mahn, right." Captain Taurus laughed. "And I can't. So I no break my eardrums trying. Virgie's man dead from bends. Old Sigh Bird on Cayman Brac, he deaf from black coral dive."

"He went down too fast?" Linda asked.

Captain Taurus shook his head. "He was greedy. He go down fine. Then he see big bush of coral just a leetle bit deeper. He go for it, and *phttt*. No more he hear."

Linda shuddered. She had nothing in her first-aid kit that could help a diver suffering from broken eardrums.

"I'll double the pay." Mars pulled some money from his billfold, but Captain Taurus just shook his huge head, grinned, and scraped his chair away from the table.

"Wait!" Mars hurried after him. "If you won't go, will you at least rent me a boat? You had two small catboats on board the *Tortuga*. Could you let me have one of them?"

"They leaky," Captain Taurus said. "Let you sink."

Mars gave up. "Let's get out of here," he said to Linda. "There must be someone on this island who'll go diving with me — someone who doesn't spoil the whole thing with a bunch of crazy rules."

When Mars paid their bill, he asked the cashier for names of divers, but the man just shook his head.

"I'll dive alone, then," Mars said as they

climbed into the car. "You'll be my buddy."

"Mars, I've no equipment except my mask and snorkel! I never dive below thirty feet."

"That's deep enough," Mars said. "You can help me into my equipment and go down your thirty feet and observe. Nothing's going to happen to me. Your uncle can stay in the boat and take care of things there. And you're a nurse. You even have first-aid equipment with you. Bring it along, if it'll make you feel safer."

"What boat?" Linda said. "Why don't you forget this idea? Everything's against it. There are other things for Uncle Sheldon to write about."

"I'm diving. I'm all the more determined to go. I have a feeling that your friend Klint is behind the scenes giving me a hard time for some reason or other."

Linda said nothing. She felt the same way Mars did. For some reason Klint didn't want Mars to dive for coral.

When they arrived at the cottage, Uncle Sheldon was still up, and Mars spoke to him.

"Mr. Burr, if you want to write about black-coral diving, you're going to have to help me out."

"I don't dive. I don't even swim."

"I know. All I want you to do is to rent a boat for us. I'm jinxed around here. Probably opened my big mouth once too often about something or other. But if you were to rent a boat, nobody would object."

"I'll see what I can do. On one condition."

Mars sighed and Linda grinned. Mars wasn't used to listening to other people's conditions.

"On the condition that we go on a ghost hunt before we go diving."

"You believe that ghost bit?" Mars asked. "You're afraid to take me diving for the coral?"

"I'm a writer. A good ghost yarn livens up any book. I don't expect to see a ghost, but my story will ring true if I can say I went to the ghost's hangout and he wasn't home. I'll rent a boat tomorrow. We'll go out tomorrow night on the ghost mission. The next day you can go diving."

Mars shrugged. "You seem to be calling the signals."

Linda was glad when Mars left, when her uncle was in bed, and when her own head hit the pillow.

There was no need to worry about

Uncle Sheldon's mood the next morning. His face was aglow; he swallowed his medicine without complaint. After breakfast he rented a boat from the McKlintocks, took a brief instructional ride, then retired to the cottage to work for the morning.

Linda didn't see Klint until the afternoon, and then they spoke only briefly.

"Mars and Uncle Sheldon and I are going on a ghost hunt tonight," Linda said with a laugh. "Uncle Sheldon wants to write it up for his book. Care to come along?"

She almost hated to ask Klint to accompany them, yet Uncle Sheldon was interested enough in the coral dive for her to be willing to hide the real reason for the boat rental.

"Thanks for the invite," Klint said. "I accept. You really should have a seaman along. It's not good for an inexperienced crew to go out at night."

At dinner that evening Mars fumed when Linda told him Klint was going with them, but when she gave her reasons, he calmed down.

"May be good thinking at that," Mars said. "At least we'll learn to know exactly how the boat operates. Your uncle can make up some excuse for keeping it another day."

After dinner Linda returned to the cottage to make sure that her uncle rested before their midnight jaunt. She knew he was too excited to sleep, but just lying down was relaxing, and she insisted that he do it.

The moon hung like a medallion high in the sky when Klint knocked on the cottage door. "Ready?" he asked.

"Mars isn't here yet," Linda said.

"Tough. Let's go without him. He's not a writer."

At that point Mars made his appearance, and his black slacks and shirt lent a mood of secrecy to their mission.

Uncle Sheldon joined them, and they walked to the dock where the boat was moored. Although the night air was soft and warm, Linda was glad she had brought a light sweater with her. She shivered from inner chills. Insects stopped chirping at their approach, and an eerie atmosphere cloaked the shoreline. The moon-silvered water lapped against the sides of the boat as Klint started the motor and guided them toward the reef.

Sea spray misted Linda's face, and she tasted the salt that clung to her lips. As the trade winds blew the odor of the motor away from her, she caught the fishy scent of the sea.

"If ghosts can hear, we're not being very subtle," Uncle Sheldon said. "Can we do without that motor?"

"After a while," Klint replied. He guided the boat to the left, and as Linda looked back, she could see only a few lights on shore pinpricking the night.

Presently Klint shut off motor and lights. Mars helped him row, and they paddled through the moonlight, their oars silently dipping into the waves.

"Let's wait here," Klint whispered, "and keep silent. Voices carry like mad across water."

Linda felt somewhat foolish as they sat still as mummies. Grown-ups are much like children, she thought. They love to create their own excitement.

They waited. And waited. Linda wriggled her toes to keep them awake. The only sound now was the slap of water against the boat. A few small clouds scudded before the moon, and the stars sprinkled the sky like shining seeds broadcast on a sable field.

Linda was so engrossed in scanning the sky that she didn't see the other boat until Mars nudged her. Her chest tightened, and she gasped as if in pain.

Far ahead of them stood the ethereal figure of a pirate in a low boat. The moon glinted on the metallic band that held a scarlet cummerbund in place, and shot sparks from silver knee buckles and from a sword that dangled from the pirate's belt. The shadow of his three-cornered hat hid his face.

"The g-ghost!" Uncle Sheldon muttered under his breath. "It's for real!"

"Ghost, my grandmother's beard!" Mars spat the words. "Give chase. That's someone we know. Give chase!"

Klint opened the motor wide, but as they sped through the water the pirate and his boat disappeared before their eyes.

Linda clung to the side of the boat, unmindful of the spray that drenched her. The boat veered suddenly to the right, and Klint cut the motor.

"No use. He's gone."

They sat there staring at the vast empty sea that revealed no trace of any boat other than their own.

"But where could he have gone?" Linda asked. "There's no place to hide."

"I've no idea," Klint said. "I'm as surprised as you are. I certainly thought we were coming out here on a fruitless chase. But I saw it. I'll never deride Virgie again.

Seeing's believing."

"Not in my book," Uncle Sheldon said. "And I mean that literally. There has to be a logical explanation for all this."

Only the sound of the motor broke the silence as they headed for shore, and when they reached the dock, Klint secured the boat and bid them good night.

"The boat'll be right here in the morning, Mr. Burr," Klint said. "From the looks of the sky it'll be a fine day for fishing or writing. Good luck to you."

Klint took off with easy strides toward his house, while Mars headed in the opposite direction. Linda and her uncle went straight to their cottage. Few words passed between them. There was nothing to say. They had gone on a ghost hunt, and they had found a ghost.

Linda had just turned the lights out and slipped into bed when someone tapped on the porch door.

"Don't put your lights on," Mars's voice hissed. "Just let me in for a minute."

Uncle Sheldon beat Linda to the door, and Mars slipped quietly onto the porch.

"If you two are planning to play Romeo and Juliet, I'd appreciate it if you'd find another balcony," Uncle Sheldon said. "The night's all but shot as it is."

"Sorry to bother you, Mr. Burr," Mars said, "but I had to talk to you, to both of you. Tonight isn't going to make any difference in our diving plans, is it? I mean, you don't believe that ghost business, do you?"

"I really don't believe it," Linda said. "But I saw it."

"Yeah, me, too," Uncle Sheldon said. "That ghost boat didn't even make any noise, yet it got clear away from us."

"It didn't seem to make any noise because our own boat was making such a racket we couldn't hear anything else." Mars leaned forward, still whispering. "I don't know what *you* think of Klint, but I think he was behind the whole ghost bit."

"I don't think so," Linda said firmly. "He was as startled as we were."

"Okay. Okay." Mars sighed. "I won't argue that point with you. I just want to know that you're going with me tomorrow."

"I think you're taking too big a risk," Linda said. "With no safety buddy, you could get into trouble. There are sharks —"

"I've got the safety angle figured out," Mars interrupted. "I'll tie a rope around my waist, and you can play it out as I dive. If I have any problems I can't handle, I'll tug on the rope, and you and your uncle can tow me to the surface."

"Sounds reasonable," Uncle Sheldon said. "But just for one deep dive. No more. All I want to know is what's down there. If you can bring up a small piece of black coral, fine. But if it's too dangerous, just come back with a description for me."

"Uncle Sheldon! You're asking Mars to risk his life for a story — for incidents for your book!"

"I'm asking no such thing," Uncle Sheldon replied. "Mars is hell-bent on diving for that coral. All I want is a description of the action."

"Stop worrying, Blondie. Everything's going to be okay. But there's just one more thing. I want to pack all the stuff we're going to take. I've borrowed a heap from the bug boys, and we can pack our gear tonight, then park the car a way from here."

"Why?" Linda asked.

"Secrecy. Tomorrow, anyone who watches us leave the dock will see nothing more unusual than a swimming and picnicking party. If we're seen loading scuba gear and first-aid equipment, the word will spread all over the island before midmorning."

"Let's do it his way," Uncle Sheldon said

to Linda. "Get your medical supplies, Nurse Carrol."

"Bring your gear out on the porch and wait for me," Mars said. "I'll go load my scuba tank and regulator."

"Have you checked it out for safety?" Linda asked.

"Did that yesterday afternoon while you and your island hero were cavorting on Cayman Brac. Be back in a sec."

Linda hurried to get the first-aid supplies. She pulled her shades down and worked by the dim beam of a flashlight, feeling all the while that both Mars and her uncle were humoring her. But humoring her was not going to discourage her. She checked over her equipment until she was sure that all was in order.

When Mars returned, he and Uncle Sheldon eased Linda's first-aid kit and snorkel and mask into the car. Then Mars drove off quietly without the aid of headlights. The whole night had been so cloaked in secrecy that Linda shuddered with unwonted fear as she dropped into bed for a few hours' rest.

Chapter Ten

It is hard to preserve a sense of mystery when the sun glows like a torch and the soft trade winds cool the earth. Linda felt totally in the here and now when she and Mars and Uncle Sheldon toted their lunch aboard the McKlintocks' boat the next morning. They all wore swimsuits, terrycloth shirts, and rubber-thonged sandals. Uncle Sheldon made a show of displaying his briefcase and notebooks, and Mars spoke in loud tones to a co-worker about bringing back water samples from various shorelines in order to test them for mosquito larvae.

Once they were on the water, Linda asked, "Where did you leave our equipment?"

"In the opposite direction," Mars said with a nod. "I want nobody to follow us or spy on us." He steered the boat into a cove and scooped up some water in one of the bottles he had brought. Then he headed across the cove to another inlet. They had been on the water for over an hour before he eased the boat into the cove where he had left his diving gear and Linda's equipment. Once these were in the boat, Mars covered them with a tarp and headed for the reef.

"Think you can find the spot where we were last night?" Uncle Sheldon asked.

"I think we're already in the general area," Mars said. "The thing we have to hunt for is the dropoff where the trench begins. I understand there's a sheer wall that drops away for miles."

"How will we ever find it?" Linda asked.

"We can dive in and take a look-see," Mars replied. "Or we can look through this glass-bottom bucket I just cleverly happened to bring along." Pulling the bucket from under the tarp, he plunged it into the water and motioned Linda and her uncle to look.

"I can see clear to the bottom," Linda said. "It's unbelievable!"

Uncle Sheldon peered through the bucket bottom for some time before setting it back down and making notes in his notebook.

"Let's take a dive right up ahead," Mars suggested. "It may not be the spot, but we might run into it accidentally."

Linda nodded. Presently Mars cut the motor, and they donned mask, snorkel, and fins. Mars went over first in a feet-first dive, and Linda followed. The water felt warm yet refreshing, and she exhaled through her nose to prevent her mask from sucking against her face as the water pressure changed.

No matter how many times Linda went diving, she never got over her initial surprise at the beauty present in the underwater world. The coral hues were fantastically beautiful in shades of purple, green, and orange. A full spectrum of colors was on display, and Linda felt as if she could stay down for hours. Only her burning lungs brought her back to the surface for air.

"What's it like down there?" Uncle Sheldon called from the boat.

"It's like a fluorescent fairyland," Linda said. "Where's Mars?"

"He surfaced and dived again," her uncle replied.

Linda submerged and watched a parrot fish, a jewel fish, and a school of ballyhoo swim to the left of her, playing hide-and-seek among the sea sponges and sea fans. When Linda surfaced a second time, Mars was ready to help her back into the boat.

"We'll come out to play another day," he said. "Right now we've got to find that trench. That's our business for today."

Once more they headed farther out to sea, and while Uncle Sheldon steered the boat, Mars and Linda peered through the bucket, hoping that the bottom of the ocean would disappear from view.

It was when they had almost given up finding the trench that Linda let out a whoop. "I think we're right over it! Take a look, Mars!"

Mars peered through the glass bucket, and his hands shook with excitement. "I think you're right. Let's check it out."

Mars was in the water first; Linda had paused to smear saliva over the lens of her face mask to keep it from fogging up. When she joined Mars, she knew they had found the right spot. The water was crystal clear, and far below them was the edge of what seemed like a wall. Then the wall ended, and the ocean bottom disappeared into nothingness.

Linda felt a warning pressure against her eardrums as she dived deeper than her normal depth. The colors were like magnets drawing her ever toward them, but her throbbing chest forced her to surface. Mars was already back in the boat, and he gave her a hand over the side.

"Okay, buddy, help me into my gear."

"Have you checked it out?" Linda asked.

"Yes, yes, I told you I had."

"But that was two days ago. Give it another going-over right now. You're taking a big enough chance just diving alone. The least you can do is to be absolutely sure your equipment is in good working order."

Mars checked gauges, regulators, straps, everything that could possibly cause trouble by malfunctioning. At last even Linda was convinced that his equipment was seaworthy.

"I'm worried about that rope, Mars," she said. "You could get all tangled up in it."

"Want me to dive without it?" Mars teased.

Linda shook her head and stepped behind Mars to hold his oxygen tank while he slipped into the harness. Once the harness and regulator were adjusted properly, Mars was ready to enter the water.

"Remember all those things Captain Taurus told you," Linda said. "You may think he's wrong, but just this once play it by the rules. Don't you dare stay down too long or go deeper than you're supposed to."

Mars could hear, but his equipment kept him from replying. From the side of the boat he did a backward roll into the water. Linda slipped into her mask and snorkel and dived after him, but Mars was soon far below her, and she had to surface for air.

"Better come back into the boat," Uncle Sheldon advised. "If Mars needs help, it might take both of us to tow him up. And you would know more about the timing than I would." He leaned over to give Linda a hand, and she heaved herself back into the boat.

She watched while the line played out farther and farther. Minutes passed. Surely Mars must be down to the two-hundred-foot depth by now. Although the water was clear, Linda couldn't see him through the glass-bottom bucket. Her mouth grew parched, and her fingernails were cutting into her palms when Uncle Sheldon shouted, "The rope! He's in trouble! What can you see?"

Linda couldn't see anything, for she had dropped the bucket and was grasping for the rope.

"I don't know how deep he is, but he shouldn't come up any faster than his slowest bubbles," she said.

"Big help when you can't see the bubbles." Uncle Sheldon eased the rope back into the boat.

"We'll measure the rope. He shouldn't come up faster than twenty-five feet per minute. You measure, I'll time."

"I can both measure and time. You get over the side and find out what ails him, if you can."

Linda needed no urging. She slipped into her mask and fins and did a head-first dive into the sea. She followed the rope down, down as deep as she dared go with only a mask. She could see Mars's form far below, and it seemed as if he was easing up inch by inch instead of foot by foot. Linda surfaced for another gulp of air, then submerged again.

This time she went deeper, and Mars had risen closer to her. Now she could see why he had signaled to them. Although she had never seen an octopus before, she knew she was seeing one now. Its bulbous body was a murky brown color, and its spindly arms were inextricably wound around Mars's head and neck.

Linda had to surface for air, but when she dived again, Mars was still at such a great depth that she couldn't reach him.

The horrid creature still clung to Mars's head, and this time when Linda came up for another breath, she paused long enough to tell Uncle Sheldon the bad news.

"I'm going down until I reach him this time," she said. "Get me the knife from the first-aid box."

Treading water until her uncle found the pocket knife and opened it, Linda then held the weapon in her teeth and surface-dived into the depths. Down. Down. She had never been so deep.

At last she could reach Mars's head. She had intended to slash at the octopus's arms with her knife, but now she knew her judgment hadn't been that sharp. There was too much danger of injuring Mars. In order not to frighten him, she swam in front of him, hoping he could see her between the grasping arms that encircled his head. Frantically she jerked at one of the tentacles.

Nausea flooded her as the tentacle broke off in her hand. She was forced to surface for air. Carrying the knife in her hand, she remembered to exhale on her way up. When her body broke the surface, she flung the knife into the boat and dived again.

Was an octopus bite poisonous? Linda

guessed that it might be. This time she didn't have to dive so far to reach Mars. Again swimming in front of him, she clutched at the ball-like body of the mollusk but couldn't dislodge it. She tore at the arms one at a time until only four of the eight remained fastened around Mars's neck.

Now she and Mars surfaced at the same time. Uncle Sheldon helped Linda into the boat, and then they heaved Mars over the side. Uncle Sheldon gasped, and Linda feared that she might have two patients on her hands. But he overcame his revulsion and helped her remove the octopus from Mars's head and pitch the writhing arms overboard.

"It oozed from a crevice in the wall," Mars gasped when Linda had helped him out of his diving gear. "My whole head feels numb."

Linda dug into her first-aid supplies, glad for the chance to turn her back so that Mars couldn't see the fear and horror that must show on her face. She had noticed a deep beaklike puncture on Mars's right cheek, and each of the many suckers on the octopus's arms had left a red circle on his skin. His whole head looked as if he might have tangled with a meat grinder.

Uncle Sheldon opened the motor wide and steered toward shore while Linda cleaned Mars's abrasions and wounds and applied disinfectant.

"We're not going in!" Mars cried in dismay. "I'm all right. I've got to dive again. I saw the black coral. It was purple at that depth. It was growing all around down there. I've got to go back!"

"Not today." Linda fought to keep her voice under control. "You know you can't make two deep dives in such a short time. Besides, I'm taking you to the hospital. That bite on your cheek needs a doctor's attention."

"It doesn't hurt," Mars said. "It just feels numb."

Uncle Sheldon steered the boat to where they had left the car Mars had borrowed, and he and Linda helped Mars from the boat and into the vehicle. Uncle Sheldon drove straight to the hospital's emergency room, where Linda felt suddenly at home among the familiar odors. She and her uncle waited in the corridor until the doctor came out to speak with them. His dark skin seemed almost ebony against the starched whiteness of his hospital jacket, and when he spoke, his voice had the velvet quality of the islands.

"Your friend is in satisfactory condition, thanks to quick action on somebody's part, but to be safe, we'll keep him overnight for observation. You may talk to him after the nurse has him settled in a room."

By the time Linda and her uncle saw Mars again, he had already seen himself in a mirror.

"I'm ruined!" he exclaimed. "And they won't even bandage anything except that cheek puncture."

"You don't look so bad now," Linda said. "And you'll heal more quickly if the air reaches your skin. Better try to sleep and forget the whole ordeal. We'll be back to see you tomorrow."

Uncle Sheldon left the room, and Linda brushed a kiss on Mars's uninjured cheek.

"Marry me," Mars said. "I need a nurse."

"You need sleep. And hush up about my being a nurse. Top secret, you know."

Linda drove Uncle Sheldon back to the boat so that he could take it to the dock, then she headed for the lodge. The news of Mars's mishap had reached the Pirates' Rendezvous before she did, and a knot of people was on hand to watch her unload the diving gear and the first-aid supplies. Klint came out to help her, and when she went inside, he followed.

"He was diving for black coral, wasn't he?" Klint asked.

"He mentioned that," Linda said, trying to be true to Mars's confidence and still not lie to Klint.

"He's lucky he didn't get into more trouble than he did. But that's his business."

Klint left so abruptly that Linda had no chance to talk to him further. Had she only dreamed that he had proposed to her? What had happened to the warmth between them? Everything seemed unreal, and she realized that she needed rest almost as badly as Mars did.

Chapter Eleven

The following day Linda awakened feeling fresh and rested, but when she went to her uncle's room to prepare his medicine, she found him still in bed.

"It's my stomach," he moaned. "Feels like someone's working inside it with a pickax."

Linda assumed her professional manner immediately. She took his temperature, his pulse, and his blood pressure, and recorded the readings on a chart she had prepared for just such a purpose.

"Everything seems normal," she said. "I suppose I let you overdo it yesterday. We were out in the boat too long — there was too much excitement."

Uncle Sheldon looked sheepish. "You're not to blame. I did this to myself."

"What do you mean?"

"Oh, I got fed up with that bland diet

you've been planning for me. After you went to bed early last night, I slipped into the dining room and persuaded Gem to fix me some hash browns and a fried porkchop. Had a tomato juice cocktail for starters. That woman's quite a cook. She told me about some of her original recipes."

"Uncle Sheldon! You didn't eat all those things. You didn't!"

"I did. And I'm paying for it. You go on about your business. I'll just lie here and be miserable."

"I'd like to do just that," Linda said angrily. "You're worse than a child. But Dr. Mercer warned me. You won't get rid of me with your run-on-and-play routine. I'm sticking right here to supervise your meals. I think we better eliminate the antibiotics for today, at least, and I'll ask Virgie to bring you cream and crackers for breakfast, lunch, and dinner. If you're good, I may let you have some gelatin or a custard between meals."

Linda's nursing duties kept her close to the cottage for the next few days. Klint stopped by to keep her company almost every afternoon while Uncle Sheldon napped or worked at his typewriter. And although Mars had been released from the hospital, Linda had seen him only once.

One afternoon Uncle Sheldon tried to give Klint and Linda an assignment. "I wish you two would talk to Captain Taurus for me. He's been ashore long enough now to be rested and ready to go out again. Why don't you visit him and see what he says?"

"Uncle Sheldon, that's not fair! You know I can't just go up to a stranger and ask such a thing."

"Your timing's bad, Mr. Burr," Klint said. "A pretty girl might be able to influence Captain Taurus to do her bidding, but only if all conditions are go. He's not going to be interested in taking a sick man on a strenuous voyage."

"Who's sick?" Uncle Sheldon demanded. "Had a little stomach upset, that's all. I'll be good as new in a few days."

"Then better wait those few days," Klint said. "Let Taurus see you in good health. And now since you're feeling so much better, you'll probably have no objection to my taking Linda for a walk for an hour or so. Right?"

"Right," Uncle Sheldon sighed.

Linda laughed when she and Klint left the cottage. "You should be looking after him, Klint. You actually make him listen to reason."

Klint smiled down at her. "You're the one I want to listen to reason. Have you thought about marrying me? I don't want to rush you into a decision. I just want to know that you're thinking about it."

"Of course I'm thinking about it," Linda replied. "How can I think of anything else? It's on my mind constantly."

"Mars has asked you to marry him, hasn't he?"

"How did you know that? Did he tell you?"

"I guessed. But as long as you're not wearing his ring, I can keep on hoping, can't I?"

"I'm wearing nobody's ring," Linda said evasively.

"That's what I'd like to change." Klint pulled her down on the sand beside him in the shade of an almond tree. "I'd like to see you wearing this ring." He reached into his shirt pocket and took out a small box that contained an ornate gold ring. Three large rubies were surrounded by clusters of pearls and diamonds.

Linda gasped as she turned it over in the palm of her hand.

"Mars is probably the diamond solitaire

type, but this is more my style," Klint said. "I hope you like it. Of course, it's stolen property."

"Klint!"

"This ring was salvaged from the reef by some of my ancestors. I'd like for you to wear it."

Linda didn't slip the ring on her finger for fear that its beauty would influence her into making a promise she wasn't ready to make. A marriage had to be based on more than a piece of jewelry.

"It's the most beautiful ring I've ever seen, Klint."

"And I'm offering it to the most beautiful girl I've ever seen."

"Give me a little more time, Klint. Just a little more."

He kissed her gently, and she was surprised at her instant response.

As they walked back to the cottage neither of them spoke, and the decision that Linda faced lay heavy on her mind and heart.

At the cottage Uncle Sheldon called her to bring him a drink.

"Are you going to marry him?" he asked when she brought it.

"What makes you think he's asked me?"

"The way you look. I've never seen you

so starry-eyed. A writer notices those things. Klint's a good boy. You could do a lot worse. Now, take Mars. He's unstable. A job-hopper, if I ever knew one. You'd never have a minute's peace with him."

"So who's hunting for peace? Mars is always doing something exciting." Linda felt irritated that her uncle had goaded her into defending the very trait in Mars that worried her the most. But before she could say another word, the subject of their conversation was with them in person. Linda marveled at how smoothly his face and neck had healed in just a few days' time.

"We're going again, aren't we?" Mars asked.

"Going where?" Uncle Sheldon said.

"Diving for the black coral, of course. You know, it really isn't black down there in the sea. It's a bright purple. Wish you both could see it."

"Uncle Sheldon really shouldn't go," Linda said. "He's been feeling poorly for the past few days."

"But I'm okay now," Uncle Sheldon said quickly. "It wasn't the diving that laid me low. It was the porkchop and the hash browns."

"I'm against going," Linda declared. "Look what happened to you, Mars. Captain Taurus told you that diving for black coral is dangerous. So you've seen it. Why not let it go at that?"

"I'm going out again." Mars's voice grated with irritation. "I may really be onto something here. That black coral is rare. It can be turned into jewelry — valuable jewelry. If you don't want to go out with me, I'll go alone. I'll steal a boat if I have to, but I'm going."

"Count me in," Uncle Sheldon said. "My book will have greater authenticity if I actually see the black coral, if I'm right there when it's brought to the surface."

"How about it, Linda?" Mars gave her a grin. "Tomorrow?"

"What can I say? I'm against the whole thing, but I'll not let either of you go out there alone. I'm here to care for Uncle Sheldon, and I've never yet shirked on a job."

Uncle Sheldon rented the boat the next day, and this time Linda knew it was useless to hide their equipment. Everyone knew where they were going and what they hoped to find.

A handful of people gathered at the dock to watch them leave. There was much good-natured joking about the pirate ghost, but Virgie was not among the jokers. Linda wondered if the head cook was reluctant to speak of the ghost, or if she was silent because Gem had stolen the breakfast scene by baking a delicious mango muffin that everybody had praised.

Just as they were ready to cast off, Klint drew Mars aside, and Linda couldn't help overhearing their conversation.

"Don't bring up more than one bush." Klint's voice carried a warning as well as an order.

"Whose law is that?" Mars demanded.

"There are no laws concerning the coral," Klint said. "I'm just telling you. Bring up only one bush."

For a moment Mars and Klint glared at each other, then Mars climbed into the boat and Uncle Sheldon started the motor. This time they took a direct route to the trench, and soon Grand Cayman was a mere speck on the horizon. Mars used the glass-bottom bucket to locate exactly where the ocean bottom dropped away, then he signaled Uncle Sheldon to cut the motor. Once again Linda helped Mars into his scuba gear and watched as he rolled over into the water. Then she dived in after him, staying down until he had become a blur in the depths.

Uncle Sheldon helped her back into the boat, and they waited in silence. Three minutes. Five minutes. Eleven minutes. The waves pounded against the sides of the boat. The sun pounded against Linda's head and shoulders. And Linda's heart pounded as the rope slackened. Mars was coming up.

She pulled the rope in foot by foot, trying to keep one eye on the water and one on her watch. She had been hauling in rope for about five minutes when Mars finally surfaced. He thrust two black coral bushes toward them and then scrambled aboard.

"You found it!" Linda cried as she helped him out of his diving gear, refraining from mentioning Klint's warning to bring up only one bush.

"There's a world of it down there," Mars panted. "I landed on this flat wall-like part of the cliff, about a hundred and seventy-five feet down. When I peered over the edge, I saw a whole forest of coral about twenty feet farther down."

Linda examined the bushlike coral, running her fingers over the trunks, which were about an inch in diameter. "I had no idea it was so big," she said. "These branches must be six or eight feet long."

"And look at these fernlike wisps." Uncle Sheldon touched the fragile ends of the branches.

"You can't imagine how much of it there is down there," Mars repeated. "I could develop a business around this coral, a business of my own! Why should I work for someone else when I could form my own company, maybe my own corporation? The possibilities are limitless!"

Linda saw people waiting for them at the dock long before she could make out their faces. When they finally moored the boat, they were greeted by a sort of subdued hush. There were more whispered comments than words spoken aloud.

"Mahn, you went deep!" Captain Taurus ran his knobby hands over one of the coral bushes. "Mahn! Mahn!"

Linda scanned the group that had come to meet them and noticed that Virgie was absent. Gem stood near Klint, wringing her hands and rolling her eyes and not saying a word, but Klint stepped up to Mars and spoke so that everyone could hear.

"I warned you to bring up only one bush." Klint's eyes flashed blue fire, and he

161

stood directly in front of Mars, blocking his way.

"I must have misunderstood," Mars said lightly. "Just thought I'd save myself a trip by bringing up two. If you claim ownership to those waters, I'll be glad to pay up."

Klint gave a snort of disgust and stepped aside, allowing Mars to pass.

Chapter Twelve

During the next few days Linda saw neither Mars nor Klint for any length of time. She waved to them in the dining hall or on her brief stroll between the cottage and the lodge, but both men seemed to avoid her. She wondered if they had made an agreement between themselves to give her ample time to reach a decision on marriage.

Linda had kept her uncle on such a bland diet that she was beginning to feel sorry for him. And she was afraid that if she didn't think of more interesting fare, he might persuade Gem to cook something else that would make him ill.

"Perhaps I could persuade Virgie to make you some of that cheese sauce like I used to make you," Linda said.

"I'm all for that," Uncle Sheldon said. "Go ask her."

"It's not that easy," Linda said. "She might say no."

"Then go tell her. Don't give her a chance to refuse."

"Virgie's the queen of that kitchen. Nobody tells her anything. Unless it's Mrs. McKlintock. And her ego's been taking a pounding lately. Gem's come up with some mighty tasty dishes."

"I wouldn't know," Uncle Sheldon replied dourly.

Linda ignored her uncle and tried to figure out how to approach Virgie about her cheese-sauce recipe. Would Virgie consider the recipe an affront to her efficiency? Would she resent Linda's interference? Linda squirmed.

When she grew conscious of her uncle's eyes upon her, she smiled and headed for the kitchen. The dining area was deserted at this time of the afternoon, and even Gem had gone home.

"Virgie?" Linda called, pushing open the swinging door.

"Come in, miss," Virgie said. "You change your mind about your uncle's dinner menu?"

"Not at all," Linda replied. "But I need your help. I have a recipe for a cheese sauce that can be served over any kind of fish, but I've used it at home so often that Uncle Sheldon is sick of it. You're such a creative cook that I was wondering if you'd have any ideas for adding something to it that wouldn't irritate his stomach but would have a unique flavor."

"Where be the recipe?" Virgie asked.

"I can tell it to you." One by one, Linda listed the ingredients for the sauce while Virgie wrote them down. When Linda finished, Virgie studied the list, her face clouded with the effort of her concentration. At last she spoke.

"We could substitute green turtle broth for part of the liquid you be using. That would give the sauce a different flavor. And I've a loaf of homemade bread I made from breadfruit. I could toast some crumbs and garnish the sauce with them."

"That sounds marvelous! But do you have time? I could help."

"Plenty of time. Cooking be my job. You just be here to taste tonight. That be your job."

Linda hurried back to the cottage. "Your menu will have some variety tonight, Uncle Sheldon. Virgie went along with my idea for the cheese sauce."

"You have more influence than you

think." He sipped at a glass of milk. "How long until dinner?"

"A few hours." Linda laughed. "Anticipation is a big part of enjoyment. You'll have the afternoon to think about it."

At suppertime Linda welcomed the chance to break away from the cottage and the typewriter, but she was unprepared for what greeted them at the dining lodge. Special hand-printed cards on each table urged the guests to try green turtle rarebit, Virgie's new specialty of the house.

Several diners were already devouring the treat, and Virgie beamed as she personally served seconds.

"I should really tell folks that I used your recipe," Virgie said as she served Linda.

"Don't you dare! I would never have thought of the broth or the crumbs. This is your original recipe."

Virgie was still receiving her compliments with grace when Linda and her uncle left the dining hall. Shortly afterward Klint appeared at Linda's cottage door to her happy surprise.

"I wanted to congratulate you on the meal," Klint said. "Virgie told me all about it."

"It was her twist to the recipe that made it a success."

"I was congratulating you on having the gumption to approach her with your idea. I know it wasn't easy for you. You did the thing you feared, and you did it by driving to the heart of Virgie's interest — her cooking."

"I wasn't thinking of being afraid. I was only thinking of Uncle Sheldon and Virgie." Linda was so glad to see Klint again that she was almost speechless. She was about to offer him a chair when Virgie appeared and asked to speak to her privately. As if on signal, Klint excused himself and hurried away.

"You do me a big favor today," Virgie said when they were alone. "I repay. You still want a turtle voyage for your uncle?"

"Oh, yes, Virgie! But I'm afraid to ask Captain Taurus about it. And Uncle Sheldon keeps putting it off until he feels better. I think he's afraid, too."

"Virgie not afraid of Taurus. You come with me now. Taurus be at the dining hall. There were leftovers, and I invited him to enjoy some rarebit. He be in a good mood. Full stomach. Now a good time to talk to him. Come. I make him listen."

Linda didn't want the responsibility of meeting Captain Taurus and presenting her uncle's request. If the captain refused,

Uncle Sheldon would be terribly disappointed.

"Let me ask my uncle to come with us," Linda said. "It would be best for him to plead his own case." Before Virgie could protest, she opened the door to her uncle's room. But it was too late. Uncle Sheldon had retired and was sleeping soundly. Linda couldn't bring herself to awaken him.

"He sleep," Virgie said. "You come."

Linda hesitated, but there was nothing for her to do but go along with Virgie's plans. She went to her room, ran a comb through her hair, and put on a dab of fresh make-up before accompanying Virgie to the lodge. Most of the lights were out, but at one table Captain Taurus sat alone, his face lighted eerily by the glow of the candle in the hurricane lamp.

"Taurus," Virgie began, "you meet Linda before, but tonight she ask a favor."

"What be it?" Captain Taurus's voice boomed through the empty hall as he rose and pulled out a chair for Linda.

Linda wished she had more time to prepare her plea, but it was too late now. All she could do was to blurt out her request.

"My uncle is writing a book," Linda explained. "You probably know that. The thing he wants most to include in it is an account of a turtle voyage."

"That be easy," Captain Taurus said. "I talk to him any time. I tell him about the turtles — about the *Tortuga*."

"That isn't exactly what he had in mind," Linda said. "He wants to sail on a turtle voyage. He wants to write from first-hand experience."

Captain Taurus was silent for several moments. "I just return from voyage. He should be here last April. I no go again until next April."

"Couldn't you go again now?" Linda asked beseechingly. "Just a sort of trial run. You really wouldn't have to catch more than one turtle as an example."

Captain Taurus shook his head, and Linda felt the chill fog of failure settle over her. She was about to leave when a crafty gleam shone out of his dark eyes.

"Your uncle willing to pay for a trip?" he asked.

"I suppose he planned to pay for his passage and mine." Linda tried not to stammer.

"Women no go on turtle voyage," Captain Taurus growled. "Never any women go."

Linda said nothing. If she told the captain that she was her uncle's nurse, she would be betraying his confidence. And she would then have revealed that her uncle wasn't in perfect health. She couldn't risk that. She pushed her chair back from the table to leave, but Captain Taurus stopped her with a glance.

"Why not bring your uncle here to talk to me? We men talk business."

"I'm sure he would be glad to talk to you," Linda said in a relieved tone. "Why don't you come to our cottage? You can sit and visit on the porch."

"I don't visit people," Captain Taurus intoned. "They visit me. Bring him here. I wait."

Linda hurried off, puzzled and upset. The first thing to be done was to awaken her uncle. Hurrying into his room, she shook him gently by the shoulder.

"Uncle Sheldon! Wake up!"

"Is it morning?" He sat up and knuckled sleep from his eyes.

"It's about ten p.m.," Linda replied. "But wake up and get dressed. Captain Taurus Gibraltar is ready to talk to you about going on a turtle voyage. And I think he means business. But it's going to cost you, and he says he never takes any women."

Once he realized the importance of the situation, he lost no time in getting dressed. "Where's Klint? Where's Mars?"

"I don't know where they are," Linda said. "Why?"

"I want them with me. Both of them. Klint knows these islands and he knows Captain Taurus, and he's a fair man. He won't let that old geezer pick my pocket. And Mars has charm. He's got a lot of things I can't stand, but he has charm. Maybe he can turn it on Captain Taurus. Go find both of them."

"No," Linda said. "I won't go running after either one."

"I'll go." Virgie spoke from the porch, where she had evidently been waiting and listening. "Taurus drives a hard bargain, and he's ready to talk business. You'll need everyone on your side you can get. I'll fetch Mr. Klint and Mr. Mars."

Virgie disappeared into the night as Linda and her uncle walked toward the dining hall. They had been there only a few moments when Virgie returned with Mars and Klint.

"The meeting grows larger," Captain Taurus said with a chuckle. "I think you all afraid of Taurus."

"I'm not afraid," Virgie said. "Not one

bit of it. You be fair with these people, or you have Virgie to answer to."

For a while everyone seemed to talk at once, Taurus and Virgie raising their voices higher and higher. During the discussion Mars moved to Linda's side.

"Someone stole my black coral," he whispered in her ear. "Any ideas?"

Linda shook her head. "I hope you don't suspect me."

"Of course not. But it could be anyone. Whoever heard of a hotel with no locks on the doors? It's surprising that any of us has anything left to our names."

Linda was about to speak in behalf of the honesty of the Caymanians, but Virgie and Taurus had grown silent and Uncle Sheldon was speaking.

"I want to sail on a turtle voyage, and I'm willing to pay," he said. "But I won't be robbed. You'll have to set a fair price."

"What you call fair?" Taurus turned his head slowly on his thick neck.

"One I can afford," Uncle Sheldon replied.

"There be expenses," Taurus said. "Must pay a crew. Must buy food. My time be worth something. And there be no turtles to pay for trip."

"Why no turtles?" Uncle Sheldon asked.

"Too late in season. As it is, we probably have to sail far south, sail to Turtle Bogue to find any catch."

"I'll crew for you." Mars spoke up. "And for free, too."

"Mars!" Linda exclaimed. "What about your job?"

"I resigned five days ago. Up until now I've been afraid to tell you."

So that was why Mars had been avoiding her. Linda was relieved and exasperated at the same time.

"I'll help crew for you, too," Klint offered, "and I think my folks will be willing to offer the trip to any of their guests who might care to go. It'd be good advertising. The business could pay part of the expense and the guests the other part."

"Virgie go as cook," Virgie said. "Gem help."

"No women." Captain Taurus pounded his fist on the table until the candle flickered.

"No Virgie, no Linda, no Gem, no trip." Virgie spoke with the voice of authority. "Who you think you get to cook? Abner ship out on freighter last week. Leo no cook. Kimo, no. Virgie cook. Gem help."

"How much is all this going to cost me?" Uncle Sheldon asked, near despair.

Captain Taurus was silent for a long while. He pulled a stub of a pencil from his pocket and drew some figures on the back of a menu. At last he tore off a corner, wrote a figure on it, and handed it to Linda's uncle.

"That be my price."

Uncle Sheldon read the figure and swallowed twice before he responded.

"I accept your offer, Captain Taurus."

"I thought you see it my way," the captain replied. "We sail day after tomorrow. Half the money due before we weigh anchor. Other half due when we return."

"I know one thing for sure." Uncle Sheldon looked directly at Captain Taurus. "Piracy isn't quite dead in these islands yet!"

"Right, mahn, right!" Captain Taurus slapped his knee and wheezed with laughter.

Linda glanced from her uncle to Captain Taurus. She had thought that she wanted the best for her uncle, but now that the matter of the turtle voyage was settled in his favor, she had many misgivings. What if her uncle had an ulcer attack miles out at sea? It was her responsibility to help keep him well, and she didn't know if she could do that under those circumstances.

Then there was the matter of the *Tortuga* itself. She had considered it picturesque when she had seen it at the turtle crawl. But its picturesqueness was partly due to its state of disrepair. She wondered if the boat was really safe.

Next in line on her worry list was her relationship with Klint and Mars. How would she manage within the confines of a turtle schooner with both of them so close at hand? Of course, she would have Uncle Sheldon to talk to, but as she thought of Captain Taurus and the other people who would make the trip, something in her shriveled, and she had that old feeling that perhaps she was invisible.

Captain Taurus snapped her out of her worrisome thoughts. "Tomorrow morning at nine o'clock I want everyone be at *Tortuga* for orders."

"We'll be there," Klint assured him. "You're anchored off the Georgetown quays?"

Captain Taurus nodded and stumped from the dining hall. Linda watched his rolling gait until he was out of sight, then she turned to Virgie.

"How can we thank you, Virgie! You made this whole trip possible!"

"You be saving your thanks till we back

safe," Virgie said. "I think turtle voyage something you never forget."

Linda and her uncle left for their cottage.

"He's robbing me," Uncle Sheldon said. "Pure robbery."

"We don't have to go," Linda told him. "You could forget the whole idea. You could write the facts from interviews with people who have gone on such voyages. It would be a lot cheaper."

"Forget that. There are times to save and times to spend. Between us we've managed to talk old Taurus into this voyage. I'll not back out now."

Chapter Thirteen

Linda slept fitfully that night, and it seemed that just when she was dropping off to sleep, it was time to get up. She could tell by the sounds from the next room that her uncle had been awake for some time. As she finished dressing, Klint stepped onto the porch. He wore his usual khakis, but his face shone with eagerness.

"If you haven't made other plans, I'll drive you to the *Tortuga*," he said. "But we should get going. Captain Taurus hates to be kept waiting."

"But we haven't had breakfast yet," Linda protested.

"Speak for yourself," Uncle Sheldon said. "I've already been to the dining room. Toast, cereal, milk, cream. It was a gastronomic adventure."

Linda ignored her uncle's sarcasm. "I suppose I can eat later. We mustn't keep the captain waiting."

"Here." Her uncle handed her some crackers. "I scrounged these from the dining hall yesterday. They'll keep you from starving."

For once glad of her uncle's frugal habits, Linda munched a cracker as they climbed into Klint's car and drove toward Georgetown. As they neared the quays the turquoise sea where the *Tortuga* rode at anchor took on a yellow glare from the blinding sunlight. Frigate birds circled above the stumps of spars that had been converted to cargo masts when the schooner had been restyled as a motor vessel. An unpainted deckhouse gave the craft a bulky, unfinished appearance.

A native boy rowed them out to the *Tortuga* in a flatboat, and when they were aboard the schooner, Linda saw Captain Taurus standing in the stern, his thick legs planted onto the salt-scoured timbers as if they had taken root. Virgie and Gem sat on a stack of scrap wood, while Kimo and Leo perched on oil drums. Linda recognized the two men, but no greeting passed between them.

"Where's Mars?" Uncle Sheldon asked quietly.

"Maybe he's belowdeck." Linda nodded

toward the hold where two men were working.

Klint shook his head. "That's the engine hold, and those men are the engineer and his helper from Jamaica. I asked Mars to ride with us, but he wasn't ready. Said he'd come later."

Captain Taurus cleared his throat, and everyone snapped to attention. Trying to ignore the dip and sway of the deck beneath her feet, Linda gazed out at where a mass of whitecaps were collecting in long ridges. The heat from the sun brought out a certain fetid odor from the boat timbers, and she tried to inhale the trade winds that carried the fresh salt scent of the sea.

Captain Taurus motioned Uncle Sheldon to stand beside him, and then he was ready to speak.

"Gentlemen and . . . ladies. This be the man who pay for this voyage. Mr. Sheldon Burr. He be boss, but I be captain. Mr. Sheldon Burr, meet our crew. Slim! Jed! On deck!"

The two Jamaicans crawled from the engine hold, and Captain Taurus continued.

"Slim and Jed be our engineers. They know their business. Good men. Next, Kimo."

Kimo rose from an oil drum, throwing

his shoulders back and his chest out like a prize fighter strutting into the ring.

"Kimo be our mate," Captain Taurus said. "Now will the crewmen stand? Leo. Klint. Mars Ramsey."

Leo and Klint stood, and just as Captain Taurus's wind-squinted eyes searched the deck for Mars, he appeared, approaching the schooner in a small boat. He climbed on deck with no apology, unaware of the captain's disapproval.

"Aboard this boat crewmen be prompt." Captain Taurus shot Mars a glance that would have withered a palm tree, but Mars merely nodded.

"Virgie and Gem be our cooks," Captain Taurus went on. "Women on ship be bad luck, but we take them this time. To-morrow crew will report at sunrise. Load boat. We sail midafternoon. Those not aboard no go with us." The captain glared at Mars again.

"Each person aboard allowed one — one — duffel bag for personal belongings. No more. Women will sleep in deckhouse. Men sleep in cargo hold. Be there any questions?"

No one spoke.

"You have fifteen minutes to inspect boat. Then everyone but crew ashore. All hands stay and work."

"You'll have to take a taxi back to your cottage," Klint said to Linda and her uncle. "Taurus'll work us all day. And he's running a light crew, so we'll be plenty busy. But come on, let me show you the boat."

Linda followed Klint over the deck, trying not to stumble on the many impediments in the way. Turtling and maintenance equipment almost hid the ancient timbers.

"Why all this wood?" Linda asked as Virgie and Gem rose and headed toward the galley.

"It's fuel for the cooking stove," Klint replied. "The galley's up ahead."

Picking her way around the woodpile and some oil drums, Linda skirted the bilge pump and a sailing catboat that lay on its side at the widest part of the deck. The galley was a small shed that Captain Taurus had lashed to the open deck. Inside, Linda saw the open wood stove where Virgie and Gem would cook.

Shaking her head in disbelief, she looked up at Klint. "Is there any place to get a drink? Where will Virgie get cooking and drinking water?"

Klint pointed to an open oil drum filled

with water. "There's part of the supply. We carry enough drums of water to last the trip."

"But that's unsanitary," Linda argued. "Look at that whitish scum on it, Klint!"

"Your uncle asked for a turtle voyage, not for passage on the *Queen Elizabeth.* No one's ever gotten sick from drinking the water aboard the *Tortuga* that I know of. It may taste a bit like diesel oil, but no harm comes of it."

"I'm going to insist that Gem boils every drop of water we use," Linda said. "Uncle Sheldon, you're not to drink that stuff unless it's been boiled. Promise me that, or I'll not set foot on this boat tomorrow."

"Shh!" Uncle Sheldon warned. "You're sounding just like a nurse. I promise. I promise. Nothing but boiled water."

Linda took a quick peek into the cargo hold and felt her stomach churn as she caught a whiff of the odors trapped there. She couldn't imagine Mars or anyone else sleeping in such a place. In comparison to the hold, the deckhouse where the women would sleep smelled like a bed of jasmine. The bunks were narrow and close together, but they seemed clean.

"How will you ever stand it down

below?" Linda asked Klint with a twinge of guilt.

"I may bring a sleeping bag to the stern deck," he said. "Of course, if Captain Taurus should catch me —"

"Visitors ashore!" Captain Taurus bellowed the order, and Linda took her uncle's arm and hurried to obey. A boy rowed them back to the quay, where they caught a taxi to the Pirates' Rendezvous.

Linda had been worried about how she would manage her life with Mars and Klint so near her. Now she only worried about how she and her uncle would survive the coming ordeal. Three to five days to get to the turtle waters, a day or two there, and three to five days to get back. It was madness to attempt such a trip, but her uncle wouldn't be talked out of it.

Checking her medicinal supplies carefully, Linda packed her first-aid kit, then the clothing for her uncle and herself. What did one wear on a turtle voyage? Something sturdy. Beyond that it didn't much matter. Even Uncle Sheldon's everyday wardrobe seemed apropos for travel aboard the *Tortuga*.

Linda's last few hours on land flew by like clouds before the trade winds. She tried to store up energy for the trip, for she doubted that she could even doze on those narrow deckhouse bunks with the *Tortuga* tossing and pitching in the brine.

Uncle Sheldon insisted that they leave the lodge early the next morning. He wanted to witness the loading of the schooner and get the feel of the activity at the quay. In a way Linda was glad to go. Any sort of action would relieve her tension.

"This trip is going to serve a double purpose," Uncle Sheldon said. "I'll get firsthand information on turtling, and I'll also have a chance to talk to the crewmen. Many hours will pass slowly; after a while the men will be glad enough to talk. I should get some top-notch human-interest material."

"Lots of luck," Linda said as they reached the quay.

They watched Kimo carry heavy packs of staples up a gangplank and onto the *Tortuga*, which was now anchored in shallow waters.

"Looks as if we're going to live on rice and beans and bread." Linda sighed. "At least that's what Kimo's loading on now."

Aboard the schooner, his leathery face appearing brown and seamed in the harsh sunlight, Captain Taurus shouted orders to his crew. He checked every item that came aboard and at the same time listened to comments and complaints from his men. He also listened to Virgie and Gem, who were not reconciled to such rudimentary cooking facilities.

Personal gear went aboard last, and Captain Taurus questioned Linda about her two pieces of luggage.

"Only one is personal clothing," Uncle Sheldon said when Linda couldn't seem to find her voice. "The other contains medicines and first-aid supplies. The medicines are necessary. I will not sail without them."

"Pass on," Captain Taurus said. "She be your money. Take medicines, if you like."

Mars was following right behind Linda, and she noticed that he carried two canvas bags. And when the captain questioned him, he lied smoothly.

"More medicines for Mr. Burr, sir. Essentials."

Captain Taurus motioned Mars aboard, and Linda scowled at his deceit but said nothing. Mars was a natty dresser and he prided himself on always looking nice. He probably needed two bags just for clothing.

Linda arranged her few belongings in the deckhouse, choosing a bunk far from

185

the ones Virgie and Gem had claimed as theirs. Although Virgie had helped her approach the captain, Linda still felt somewhat uneasy around her. How could she truly warm up to someone who believed in pirate ghosts? And just recently she had heard rumors that Gem practiced some ancient form of witchcraft. Linda felt a need to keep her distance from the two women.

As the crew rushed forward to weigh anchor, Uncle Sheldon approached Linda.

"Will you help me take notes on all this?" he asked. "I'll dictate, and you jot down as much as you can of what I say."

"Where's a notebook and pen?" Linda asked.

Uncle Sheldon looked crestfallen. "It's in the hold with my things. Don't you have something up here? If I go back down, I'll miss some of this scene."

"I'll get it for you. You stay here and observe. I'll take my flashlight and be right back."

Linda squeezed between the galley and a catboat and hurried to the hold. She gulped a deep breath of sea air, then climbed down into the depths below. The motion of the boat made her clutch at anything that would help her keep her balance. She breathed again. Once she got used to the smell, it wasn't as bad as she had thought it would be.

Where were her uncle's things? Linda glanced around, searching for the familiar battered suitcase her uncle had carried aboard. It was nowhere in sight. As she flashed her light about, a putrid stench reached her nostrils. For a moment she ignored it, but its intensity grew, and she began poking around for its source. The hold was dark and her flashlight beam was weak, but she spotted a small box that seemed near the source of the stench.

Pressing the flashlight against her side with her elbow, she used both hands to open the box. For a moment she couldn't believe what she was seeing; then the reality became all too clear. The three-cornered hat, the crimson cummerbund, the silver knee buckles! Quite by accident she had stumbled upon the costume worn by the "pirate" they had seen on their midnight ghost hunt.

Linda dropped the lid of the box as if it had burned her hand, and then she saw the name lettered on the carton. "Klint McKlintock."

Linda sat down, too stunned to think clearly. Klint had been the pirate ghost.

No. No. Klint had been with them. But he must have had something to do with the ghost scene, for here was the evidence with his name tagged right on the box.

How long she sat there, she didn't know. But presently she realized that the stench she had smelled earlier was coming from the very duffel bag she was sitting beside. Without regard for someone's personal property, she opened the bag, flashed her light inside, and gasped.

"The black coral!" She hadn't realized she had spoken aloud until the sound of her voice startled her. Mars's black coral was right here in this bag smelling up the hold of the *Tortuga*! Was Klint responsible for this, too? Why would he steal Mars's coral? And why would he try to hide such a stench in the hold of the turtler?

Nothing made sense.

Chapter Fourteen

The impact of discovering the pirate costume and Mars's black coral left Linda so shaken that she could hardly answer her uncle when she heard him calling her.

"Linda! Are you down there? Can't you find my things?"

"Coming, Uncle Sheldon." Hurriedly she found his bag and removed a note pad and a pencil from his attache case. The pitching of the boat slowed her ascent from the hold, and when she stood again on the deck, she inhaled deeply of the salt air.

"What took you so long?" Uncle Sheldon asked. "We're missing out on things."

"There's no electricity down there. I had to find my way with a flashlight. And the smell! You won't believe it."

"Captain Taurus didn't promise a luxury liner," Uncle Sheldon said dryly. "Come on up front and take some notes for me."

Linda tried to hurry to the bow, but she found herself frantically clutching for support as the schooner rolled and dipped.

"Jot this down," Uncle Sheldon said. "We're passing from Grand Cayman's lee into the whitecaps of the open ocean. We're using a fores'l and job in addition to the engine to gain a few extra knots of speed. To our starboard a skeleton of an old wreck sticks up through the choppy water like some petrified sea monster."

Linda wrote jerkily, trying to record all her uncle's words, but she couldn't help sneaking a peek at the sunken ship. The wind blew the engine noise astern, but the smell of diesel fumes swirled in the salt air, and the vibration underfoot made Linda's feet tingle.

Looking over her shoulder, she saw the buildings of Georgetown fade into the distance until the town looked like a painting done in blurred pastels. But it wasn't until she overheard the two Jamaicans speaking that she knew they were really at sea.

"De land sunk out already?" one engineer asked.

"It be," replied his partner. "We headed sout' now."

Linda stared at the Jamaican for several

moments before she realized that the mis-shapen outline of his face was caused by a wad of tobacco in one cheek.

"Get this down, Linda." Uncle Sheldon's voice snapped her from her own observations. "The natives comprising the crew are dressed in thatch hats and faded knee-length dungarees."

"Shall I mention that they're bare-footed?" Linda asked.

Uncle Sheldon nodded. "And add that Captain Taurus wears sneakers, faded chinos, and a white T-shirt, while Klint, dressed in khakis and a visor cap, looks like the true captain of the schooner. You might note that Mars appears to have es-caped from some yacht club in his navy blue double knit and white commodore's hat." Uncle Sheldon laughed. "This is what an author might call a motley crew if he were given to using cliches."

Now that there was nothing around them to see except water and a few flying fish, Uncle Sheldon took over the note-book, relieving Linda of her secretarial du-ties.

She headed for the galley, but the rolling of the boat caused her to change her mind. Instead, she went to her bunk in the deckhouse and searched through her first-aid kit until she found a bottle of motion-sickness pills. She took one, forcing herself to swallow it without water, then brought the bottle to her uncle.

"No need," he told her. "I'm not going to be sick."

Using the pills as an excuse, Linda walked around the obstacles on deck until she found Mars astern near the woodpile.

"Didn't know the crew had to keep up the galley fire," Mars muttered through clenched teeth.

"Hope you're building one big enough to allow Virgie or Gem to boil our drinking water. Mars, don't drink a drop that hasn't been boiled." Linda studied Mars and decided that he looked green around the lips and nose.

"You're sounding like a nurse," Mars said. "Old Captain Taurus would probably become mortally ill if he swallowed anything as pure as boiled water."

"Well, you don't have his iron constitution, and I recommend boiled water. Do you need a motion-sickness pill?"

"No, Nurse. All I need is a strong back. This wood is heavy."

"Mars, I have to talk to you. It's important."

"Ship sprung a leak? Dibs on being in

your lifeboat!" Mars grinned, then scowled as a splinter snagged his pants.

"Mars! Really, I have to talk to you — someplace where we won't have to shout above the engine noise."

"I'll deliver this wood to Virgie and Gem and meet you up front, okay?"

Linda nodded and made her way cautiously back to the bow, where anchor and chains clogged the deck. Her stomach felt queasy and the whole world seemed to be rolling, but gazing at the dark blue line where sky and sea met had such a restful effect that it almost hypnotized her before Mars appeared.

"What's up?" Mars asked. "If you've forgotten your hankie, I'll gladly swim back for it."

"I found your black coral. It's in the hold right on this boat. Someone on this schooner must have stolen it, but why they'd hide it here is more than I can understand. What do you think?"

"I've read about nurses who are also detectives," Mars said, "but you better stick to being a nurse-secretary. I know the coral's here. I brought it aboard. But how did you find it?"

"*You* brought it aboard! But you said someone had stolen it from you!"

"Right. But I found it. I found it hidden in a jute bag at the Pirates' Rendezvous, behind the McKlintocks' carport. I wasn't taking any chances on having it stolen again. There was no time to install a lock on my cottage door, so I just brought the coral along. How did you happen to find it?" he repeated.

"I was in the hold getting something for Uncle Sheldon when I smelled this horrible odor. I decided there was something unsanitary aboard, so I investigated."

"I thought the natural smell of that hold would mask almost any other," Mars said. "Good thing you found it and not someone else. Eventually I'll treat it with a chemical solution to remove the odor, but I haven't had the opportunity so far."

"You're going to have to do *something* with it," Linda said. "The crew may stage a mutiny if they have to share quarters with such a smell. Wrap some more stuff around it."

"What sort of stuff? All I've got are my clothes."

Before Linda could answer, Virgie rang a gong that summoned everyone to the galley. When the crew and the passengers had assembled, Captain Taurus made an announcement.

"The *Tortuga*'s day be from sunrise to sunset. Now we eat. Then we sleep. Tomorrow another day. Rest up for it."

Linda wasn't hungry, but she felt as if a load had been lifted from her when she realized that Klint hadn't been the one who had hidden the coral aboard. Yet another part of her mind was still heavy with the knowledge of the pirate costume.

Why had Klint tried to deceive her? Or was she only judging him on circumstantial evidence? It was possible that he had nothing to do with the pirate outfit. It was possible that someone else had brought it aboard and put it in the box bearing Klint's name. It was possible, but not probable. Linda's head was willing to reason, but her heart refused. Her heart tended to forgive anything that Klint might have done or might do.

Virgie's meal ran heavily to carbohydrates — beans and bread — and a brew of coffee so strong that it would almost keep its shape without the aid of the tin cups she served it in. Virgie and Gem were both dressed in starched print dresses, and while Virgie worked like a stoic, Gem fluttered about the galley like a dove trapped in a box. The meal was served on tin plates, and Linda hated the metallic flavor that clung to her beans. But she forced herself to eat, and it was only when she was finished that she noticed Mars was absent.

"Last time I saw him he was astern feeding the fish," Uncle Sheldon said in answer to her question. "Guess he hasn't found his sea legs yet."

"I offered him a motion-sickness pill, but he refused it."

"Naturally," Uncle Sheldon replied. "To have taken it would have been to live by the rules."

"You didn't take one, either," Linda retorted, wondering why she always felt a need to defend Mars even when she knew he was in the wrong.

"But I'm not seasick," he pointed out. "Mars turned that green hue the moment he stepped aboard."

After their meal Linda didn't embarrass Mars by hunting for him. She was standing alone in the bow, staring at an inverted bowl of sky and trying to figure out which star was the North Star, when Klint joined her.

"It's that one." He pointed to a bright glow overhead. "We just lined up the sternpost with the North Star to see if the compass was working correctly."

"And was it?" Linda tried to keep the apprehension from her voice.

"The compass is okay, but the radio's on the blink. Captain Taurus isn't worried, though. These old sea captains sail by luck and the grace of Neptune."

"It's already dark," Linda said. "When will he turn on the lights?"

"What lights?" Klint laughed. "Captain Taurus uses no running lights on the *Tortuga*, and if you think that's bad, you ought to know that the helmsman can't even see the sea or the stars now that the new deckhouse has been added. It blocks his view completely."

"But he has the compass, doesn't he?"

Klint nodded. "I hope he'll be able to read it by his kerosene lamp."

"No electricity anywhere?" Linda became more and more concerned over the lack of safety features on the *Tortuga*.

"There's a bulb rigged to a generator. It's used by the engineer at the engine hatch."

Linda talked with Klint for a long time, wondering if he might bring up the subject of the costume she had found in the hold. She even mentioned the ghost-pirate episode, hoping it would elicit more information, but Klint revealed nothing.

Linda had sensed a secretive quality about Klint before, but she had never been able to pinpoint it as definitely as she did now. She always had the feeling that Klint knew more about her than she knew about him. She sensed a point of mental rapport beyond which she could not go. Klint's arms about her warmed her shoulders, but there was a chill in her heart that could not be ignored. She was glad Klint didn't bring up the subject of marriage, for she was still uncertain. A part of her leaped out to him, but another part shied away and warned her to be wary.

When she awakened the next morning, the sun was just brushing the clouds with pink and gold. Gem and Virgie had already been asleep when she had come into the bunkhouse the night before, and now they were up and at work in the galley. Linda dressed in Bermuda shorts and a shirt, and when she stepped on deck, the sun was turning the sea the color of molten slag.

Virgie and Gem served a sweet, heavy johnnycake for breakfast that tasted strangely of chemicals, and Linda noticed that Mars swallowed nothing but some of Gem's strong black coffee. She made sure that her uncle drank only a mixture of powdered milk with his johnnycake.

"Look at all the birds," she said. "That must mean land is near."

"Captain Taurus says we're never too far from land," her uncle remarked. "But he says these swallows and egrets may have come from as far away as Chile."

"You've talked to him?"

"Of course. And so far he hasn't bitten me, not even once. Some flying fish sailed aboard during the night. That bulb at the engine hatch attracted them. Captain Taurus is going to use them for bait to catch fresh fish for our dinner."

"At least that's on your diet list," Linda said. "If Virgie fries it, you'll just have to scrape the crust off and eat only the tender meat."

Uncle Sheldon sighed.

Linda watched a swallow perch on the rim of an oil drum and dip its head to drink.

"That's our water supply," Klint said, coming along just then. "Captain Taurus always shares it with the birds."

Linda felt her stomach muscles tighten as she walked over to the drum. A hole had been chopped in its top, and inside, Linda saw a whitish scum on the surface of the liquid. Turning from the revolting sight, she made her way to the bow and settled down among the anchor chains to observe Kimo and Leo prepare turtle nets.

The men checked for weak spots in the wide-woven mesh of the fifty-foot nets. Since the mesh was so large, the nets were light. Neither man had to struggle to lift them. When they were sure that a net was in usable condition, Kimo secured one end of it to a buoy of wood that was anchored to a chunk of coral.

"How do those nets work?" Linda asked Klint as he passed by.

"The killick holds it in place after it's been thrown overboard," he said. "Then it floats in the current and changes position with the change of the tide. The floats along the surface side hold the net up, but the bottom side isn't weighted. The idea is for a turtle to strike it and become entangled."

Linda had more questions, but Klint had work to do. Captain Taurus kept his crew busy tending the schooner or fishing or preparing nets or sails for the catboats, and Linda had little chance to talk to either Klint or Mars. Uncle Sheldon had taken a motion-sickness pill and retired to a chair in the galley, and the old feeling of invisibleness surrounded Linda once more. She felt like a secret observer. No one spoke to her or paid her any attention, and she sensed that it was going to be a long voyage to the Miskito Bank where the green turtles sometimes played, and even a longer voyage to Turtle Bogue, where Captain Taurus believed the turtle would not be congregated.

Chapter Fifteen

Somehow the long hours passed, and Linda became used to the roll of the schooner. Her uncle, however, suffered from seasickness, and Linda guarded his diet as carefully as she could under the circumstances. He ate little. His meals consisted mostly of small portions of boiled rice or beans. Sometimes he could tolerate powdered milk or a bit of fish. Linda ate plenty of bananas because she considered them the most sanitary food available.

Uncle Sheldon didn't seem to mind his seasickness as much as he minded being unable to chat with the crew. He begged Linda to do this for him, but she couldn't bring herself to approach any of the men.

The damp, fetid air of the hold aggravated her uncle's cough, and Linda insisted that he be allowed to sleep on a bedroll spread on the galley floor. Linda's demands for her uncle's well-being didn't endear her to either Virgie or Gem, but whenever she had to approach them on some matter, she pretended that she was wearing her nurse's uniform. Then the words would come easily, and her wishes were usually granted.

On their third day at sea Captain Taurus announced that they were on the Miskito Bank, and with his announcement came other information that kept Uncle Sheldon busy taking notes.

"It be our duty to register with customs officers of Nicaragua," Captain Taurus said. "We pay port fee. Then we pay fee for each turtle caught. Pay at Cape Gracias."

"Whom do we pay?" Linda asked Klint, who had come to stand beside her near one of the catboats. "And how and when?"

"We be about one mile from river," Captain Taurus said, giving Klint no chance to speak. "I go ashore with two of crew. We pay. Mr. Burr may go along to get book-writing things if he want."

Captain Taurus chose Klint and Mars to accompany him in one of the catboats, and Kimo and Leo began to ready the craft for action.

"Linda, you're going to have to do this for me," Uncle Sheldon said, making his way to Linda's side. "I'm in no condition to take a jaunt in one of those catboats. My stomach's queasy, and I'm weak. You go and take notes for me."

"Uncle Sheldon! Mars and Klint can fill you in on what happens. I can't go. I won't know what sort of notes to take."

"I want you to go and write down what you see," he insisted. "Bring in lots of sensory perception whenever you can."

"Captain Taurus won't want me in the catboat," Linda said. "He didn't even want me on the schooner."

"She be right," Captain Taurus said, overhearing Linda's words. "No women in catboat."

"No women in catboat, no money at end of trip," Uncle Sheldon said.

Captain Taurus's neck grew red and his eyes bulged a bit, but he backed down. "Linda goes."

Leo and Kimo lowered the catboat into the sea, and Captain Taurus boarded it first. Mars dropped over the side next. Captain Taurus eyed Mars's Bermuda shorts and matching knee socks, but he said nothing.

Klint helped Linda off the *Tortuga*, squeezing her hand to give her courage as the catboat dipped in the swells. With sails set, the captain steered the boat toward shore, but Linda soon realized that something was wrong.

"Why aren't we moving?" she whispered to Klint.

"Tide's out," Klint replied. "We'll have to drag her across the bar to the river."

At Captain Taurus's command, the three men splashed overboard. Klint motioned Linda to stay in the boat, but after a few moments of watching the men try to drag the boat through the shallows, she crawled overboard to help. The water felt cool, but the shifting sand sucked at her feet, and she could hardly keep her balance.

Once they had tugged the boat across the sandbar, they found that the river was so shallow that they had to pull it upstream. Linda welcomed the breeze that broke the humidity and discouraged the mosquitoes, and she was glad that Uncle Sheldon had not tried to make this trip. She hadn't had a chance to make any notes yet, but hundreds of impressions were etched in her memory.

"I'll never forget this jungle all around us," Linda said to Klint as they stopped to rest. "But tell me about these birds."

Klint brushed the sweat from his forehead and ran his fingers through his hair, which was pasted in damp ringlets against his head.

"That's a big order. Those lazy, slow-moving ones are ibis. The ones near the shore are spoon-bills, and the egrets are heading upriver."

"What's that one?" Linda pointed to a flash of color that shot across their line of vision.

"I'm not sure. But these tropical rivers are always full of exotic hawks. It might have been a hawk."

After a few minutes' rest, Captain Taurus led them forward. Sometimes they trudged through sand, and sometimes they sank over their knees in mud. Mars had been glum and silent for most of the distance, and now he spoke up.

"I've had it, Captain. How about telling the big brass at Nicaragua no dice? We'll fish now, pay later. This is an adventure in futility." Mars slapped at a mosquito on his neck, then pulled a leech from his ankle.

Linda quickly inspected her feet and ankles, but no leeches clung to her flesh.

"The captain give orders on this voyage," Captain Taurus said, his voice bull-like and bellowing. "I say we pay now, fish later."

Only after Captain Taurus spoke did

Linda see the twinkle in his eye and realize that perhaps he wasn't as gruff as he pretended. Or perhaps he was as much of a rule-breaker as Mars.

Klint didn't argue with the captain's decision, but the trek back to open water was no less strenuous than the struggle inland had been. When they came around a bend in the river and saw the *Tortuga* at anchor, it was almost dusk, and Linda thought she had never seen such a beautiful craft in all her life.

They made it back to the schooner after another hour's struggle, and once aboard, Linda was content to retire to the deckhouse without supper. But her uncle would stand for no such nonsense. He allowed her to rest for a while, but before she retired for the night, he recorded her impressions of the inland journey, asking questions, probing, prodding her memory. The simple task exhausted him, and Linda worried increasingly about his health.

She overslept the next morning, and by the time she made an appearance, the sun was brassy and high and Kimo and Leo were again lowering a catboat into the sea.

"We're not going to try for Cape Gracias again, are we?" Linda asked Klint.

"No. The men are going out for turtles."

"Why Kimo?" Linda asked. "Why not Captain Taurus?"

"The captain prefers to stay aboard the schooner since this isn't a real turtle hunt. Usually both catboats go out, but this time he's sending only one. Kimo's the pilot. See how they're loading the nets? Kimo will decide where to set them."

Within moments the catboat masts were raised and the sails spread. Captain Taurus shouted to Kimo, "Watch for the white holes."

"What are white holes?" Linda asked Klint, hoping her uncle was getting all this down in his notebook.

"They're circular spots of open sand that are found among the coral," Klint explained. "The turtles seek out such spots, but I doubt that we'll see any turtles before we move on south."

"I see a turtle right now. Look!" Linda pointed. "It looks like a round cork bobbing in the waves."

"We may be in luck after all."

Once Kimo and Leo were in the catboat, Klint went forward to help Mars set it free. As it scudded away, the wind was so strong that Kimo had to reef the sails.

Klint had been wrong about their luck. Many hours passed before the catboat sailed back into view, but when Kimo and Leo came within shouting distance, everyone knew they had no turtles aboard. Uncle Sheldon was disappointed, but he cheered up when Captain Taurus ordered the schooner on toward the Turtle Bogue area.

The next day Linda saw a green turtle floating on the surface even before Klint pointed it out to her. Mars was so excited that he yelled right along with the rest of the crew. Virgie watched quietly, but Gem fluttered about the deck, getting in everybody's way until Captain Taurus ordered her into the galley. They hadn't had to travel as far as Captain Taurus thought they might, and everyone was in high spirits.

"I'm going with them today," Uncle Sheldon told Linda. "I can't miss out on this."

"Are you sure you feel up to it?" Linda asked.

"I've kept my last three meals down," he said. "Nothing could make me feel bad today. You want to come along?"

Linda didn't want to go, but she knew she must. If her uncle became ill, neither Kimo nor Leo would know what to do.

"What will Captain Taurus say?" she asked.

"Captain Taurus will say that money talks." Uncle Sheldon winked at her.

"Where are the nets?" Linda noticed that the bulky mesh was neither on deck nor in the catboat.

"Klint told me that Kimo and Leo set them last night." Uncle Sheldon flipped through the pages of his notebook. "Here it is. Klint said that the big greens are vegetarians. They feed on algae and seaweed and such during the day, but at night they return to some favorite refuge, perhaps under a coral head or a reef. The men set the nets in some of these likely spots, and they'll check them out this morning."

Linda felt a mounting excitement as she went into the deckhouse and put on sturdy denims and tied a red scarf about her hair. She was excited at the prospect of seeing a turtle catch, and she thought that being away from Mars and Klint for a few hours would in itself be relaxing. But she was wrong. Sailing in such a fragile craft on such a large sea was frightening.

Linda was still waving to Mars and Klint on the deck of the *Tortuga* when Kimo swung the catboat into the wind. They scudded across the water at a terrifying speed, but after traveling a short distance, the water became rough. Leo lowered the sails, and he and Kimo rowed with giant-size oars to the first place where they had set a net. Linda looked over her shoulder and saw the *Tortuga* far behind them. Then she gasped and nudged Uncle Sheldon. Ahead of them a huge creature was splashing in a net.

"We've got one already!" she cried.

Kimo swung over to the bow of the boat. Linda knew he had heard her, but he gave no sign. Even in the confines of the catboat Kimo had a way of making her feel invisible.

"It be a no-good loggerhead," Kimo shouted to Leo. "But over there. That one be a turtle."

Leo guided the boat alongside the net, and the turtle sounded. After a few minutes it surfaced again, thrashing and blowing.

Within moments Kimo and Leo brought the turtle into the catboat, and as they turned it on its back, Linda cried out:

"It's marked. Look! There on the underside!"

"It be Captain Taurus's brand," Kimo said, looking from the turtle to Linda's uncle.

"You mean Taurus has caught this turtle before?" Uncle Sheldon asked, stupefied.

Kimo and Leo nodded. "We crawled that turtle on Grand Cayman the last time the *Tortuga* came in."

"But how did it get here?" Linda forgot her shyness and looked directly at Kimo.

"She swim," Kimo said. "Maybe three, four hundred miles. She swim in two weeks, maybe. Come back home."

"How did it get out of the crawl?" Uncle Sheldon asked.

"This turtle tell us a bad storm hit Grand Cayman," Leo said. "If crawl be flooded by storm seas, turtles may escape."

Linda was almost sorry to see the turtle hunt end so swiftly, but Captain Taurus had given orders for his crew to return with their nets after they had caught one green one. The green was aboard, and now Kimo and Leo rowed to the other settings and brought in their nets, which were empty for the most part. Here and there a loggerhead had become entangled in the mesh, and the crewmen gave them a wide berth while releasing them into the sea.

"Loggerhead no vegetarian," Kimo said in answer to Uncle Sheldon's question. "Snap off finger or toe of careless turtler."

Linda held on to the side of the boat as they sailed downwind to the schooner. Kimo brought the catboat alongside the

Tortuga with a flourish of sea spray. The turtle was loaded onto the salt-cured schooner deck with a block and tackle, and Linda had the peculiar sensation of coming home as she boarded the larger craft.

The wind had freshened, and before Linda could reach the shelter of the deckhouse, the sunlight had turned a murky yellow-green and the sea looked like mud. She didn't have to be told that they were caught in a sudden squall.

Chapter Sixteen

Had the schooner's radio been working, they might have been warned of the approaching storm, but now its pounding force was upon them. The *Tortuga* shuddered under the buffeting of the wind and the steep, rolling waves.

The sun still shone through an encroaching haze, but gradually it disappeared and the sky turned a glittery gray. Each moment the wind grew stronger. Overhead, racing clouds scudded ahead of the wind, and the sea was alive and dancing with whitecaps.

Captain Taurus shouted orders to his crew as the waves washed over the salt-hardened deck. Kimo and Leo closed the hatches, and the two Jamaicans swore at the engine, which had ceased to function. Captain Taurus and Klint took turns manning the bilge pump, which had to be operated manually.

Linda glanced around in time to see Mars disappearing into the hold. Virgie was helping Uncle Sheldon to the dubious safety of the galley. Linda started to join her uncle, hardly able to make her way across the slippery deck. Rain fell in torrents, and above the crashing, thrashing sea a high wailing penetrated into Linda's consciousness. From the corner of her eye she saw Gem standing in the doorway of the deckhouse, crying out and waving her arms in a futile supplication to the sky.

For a moment Linda was torn between going to her uncle or to Gem. But she knew her uncle was with Virgie, and she doubted that he was as terror-stricken as Gem. Linda headed for the deckhouse.

The wind tore at her hair and clothing, and she couldn't take a step without clutching at something for support. Driving rain and surging waves slickened the deck, and she grasped at air as she felt her feet slip from under her. A wave washed over her, and her mouth and nose were filled with brine. Choking and spluttering, she felt herself sliding across the deck as the schooner pitched into a deep trough in the sea. Her feet and legs went over the edge, and she knew she was being washed overboard. Then suddenly she was suspended in time and space. Strong arms grasped her under her armpits and tugged her back to safety.

Klint leaned over her, water streaming from his hair into her face, but she barely noticed. She clung to him in terror.

"I was trying to get to the deckhouse," she shouted into the roar of the storm, but Klint didn't hear her. "Deckhouse!" she shouted again.

This time Klint shook his head. From somewhere he brought out a rope, and wasting no words in explanation, he tied one end around her waist in a slipknot and lashed the other end to one of the mast stumps. She felt him give her a pat on the shoulder, then he fought his way back to the bilge pump.

The wind had taken on an ugly whine, and Linda wrapped her arms around the mast for additional support. Clearly, she was here to stay. There was no hope of reaching the shelter of the deckhouse or the galley. The thrusting, beating sea pounded unmercifully at the boat, and all at once a loud crash reverberated above the other storm sounds. Instantly Linda saw what had happened. Rotten ropes, which had immobilized the unused boom, had broken, and the heavy timber had swung across the deck and crashed into the deckhouse. Linda flung water from her eyes just in time to see Kimo go down as the boom grazed his head.

The pitch of the boat flung Kimo toward the deckhouse; then the deck tilted in the other direction, and the unconscious mate slid toward the sea.

"Klint!" Linda screamed, knowing all the while her voice would never be heard. She had to act. Flinging herself onto her stomach, she reached out and grabbed Kimo's arm. The rope around her waist pulled taut, holding both of them from the raging waters.

Twisting and writhing, Linda managed to get a firm grip on Kimo, but she could not manage to pull him back to the mast. They sprawled on the deck, totally dependent on the life-saving rope Klint had rigged.

How long could she hold on? Linda's arms ached from the tremendous weight of Kimo's body; she felt as if they would be torn from their sockets. But gradually a numbness spread over them, easing the pain. Linda was afraid that the numbness might cause her to relax her grip and drop Kimo into the sea, and she forced herself to hang on.

She had read stories about storms that stopped as abruptly as they had started, but not so with this one. After what seemed like hours, the wind gradually lessened, the sky grew brighter, and little by little the angry sea calmed down. But every time Linda thought the squall had subsided, it would renew its force and beat relentlessly against the boat. When at last it did stop, Linda had almost lost consciousness.

"You can let go now. Linda! Let Kimo go. I have him. Can you stand up?"

Klint's voice in her ear gave her the will to open her eyes, and when she realized that the storm had subsided, she managed to pull herself to her knees, then to her feet. The clouds were breaking into mounds that looked like greenish-purple gelatin, and thin rays of sun streaked onto the *Tortuga.*

"Your first-aid supplies," Klint said. "Where are they? We need them badly. But first let's get Kimo to the deckhouse."

Although her arms were still numb, somehow Linda found the strength to help Klint tow Kimo to a narrow bunk and ease him onto it. Then Klint led her to the galley, which, miraculously, was still standing. She was relieved to see that

Virgie and Uncle Sheldon were unharmed, and at Klint's insistence she forced herself to swallow a cup of cold coffee. It smelled of diesel fuel, but her head cleared and her nurse's training came to the fore. She knew what she had to do.

"My first-aid supplies are in the deckhouse," she said to Klint, forgetting her own fatigue. "Bring anyone who is injured in there. I'll do what I can to help."

She hurried to the deckhouse and washed her hands with surgical soap and some salt water that had collected in an empty tin. One by one, Klint brought the injured to her.

Gem had suffered cuts from flying glass, and although she wailed and cried, Linda treated her wounds with antiseptic and bandaged the worst of them.

"Take her to the galley," Linda said to Klint. "She'll upset the others with her carrying on."

Kimo had regained consciousness, and Linda made a compress for the lump on his head, administered aspirin for the pain, and ordered him to keep on his feet, to keep walking.

She treated Captain Taurus for a gash on his arm that required a tourniquet to stop the bleeding; then she removed deeply imbedded splinters from Klint's hands and treated Leo for rope burns and facial injuries.

The Jamaican engineers had weathered the storm without mishap, but Linda glanced around, suddenly apprehensive. "Where's Mars? I didn't see him at any time during the storm. Klint! Where is he?"

"Relax," Klint sighed. "Your friend rode out the storm down in the hold. He's badly frightened but uninjured."

When everyone had been cared for, Linda fell onto a bunk and slept until her uncle awakened her.

"Better come eat," he advised. "Virgie's managed to cook some rice. Anything'll taste good when you're starved."

Linda ate and felt better. Klint begged her to rest, but she insisted on visiting each of her patients. Only now they didn't seem like patients. Sometime during the last few hours they had become people, people in whom she was genuinely interested.

"But they don't need you now," Klint argued.

"I know," Linda said, "but I need them. I'm not afraid any longer, Klint. I can make them my friends. I have lots of things to talk to them about, and I don't need a uniform to hide behind. When I was treating them, they didn't know I was a nurse. They accepted me for myself, a person wanting to help. I have more to say to each of them."

"Then I won't discourage you." Klint smiled. "Go to it."

Linda approached each crew member without hesitation, with no fear of being snubbed. She spoke to Kimo about turtling, listening to his opinions and offering a few of her own. When she talked to Leo, she showed him a lanyard that she had square-braided and asked what he thought of using that type of braiding on the rope he made.

Virgie and Gem were unhurried in their discussion of recipes when Linda turned the conversation that way, and before she left them, they had made plans to design colorful turtle-shaped aprons to wear in the dining hall of the Pirates' Rendezvous.

Linda felt a few butterflies inside her as she approached the formidable Captain Taurus, but she didn't hesitate.

"I've been thinking about that turtle we caught," she began. "Not just its size, but the fact that you caught it before and that it escaped and came back to the same spot in a relatively short time."

"Come to nesting ground to lay eggs," Captain Taurus said.

"But the turtle *knew* where to come! It's amazing. Animals have an instinct for procreation and self-preservation. It's like a success instinct that's preset. It makes me think that man has been cheated."

Captain Taurus was silent for so long that Linda was afraid that in her newfound confidence she had either bored him or said something to offend him. But when he spoke, he surprised her with his penetrating thought.

"Man not be cheated. Man have the same success instinct of the turtle and more. The turtle, as you say, has preset instinct. His goals be chosen for him. Man, he select his own. That be the great thing. Man can select his own goals."

When Linda looked deep into Captain Taurus's eyes, he squirmed, as if embarrassed to have been caught thinking serious thoughts. "I have a goal," he said with a grin. "Goal be to get this schooner back to Georgetown. Fahst, mahn, fahst!"

After Linda finished visiting with the captain and the crew, she went forward and sat alone in the bow, staring thoughtfully into the star-studded night. She wasn't surprised when Klint joined her.

She had talked to almost everyone except him, and she knew that she was merely delaying what had to be said. There had been a coldness between them ever since the first day of their voyage when she had found the pirate costume in the hold. Now that she had discovered the key to talking to people, she determined to use it well. She could never build a life with Klint unless there was honesty between them.

"Why did you try to scare us with the ghost-pirate scene, Klint? I've got to have an answer."

"How did you know?"

"I found the costume in the hold. Not a very clever hiding place."

"It's a long story." Klint perched on the anchor.

"I've got lots of time," Linda said. "Give."

"I had two reasons for doing it," Klint said. "I'm very fond of the Cayman Islands, you know. I'd like to see them even more prosperous than they are, and to my way of thinking, prosperity will come as more tourists arrive."

"You say you want tourists, yet you tried to scare Uncle Sheldon, Mars, and me away. That makes no sense."

"I wasn't really trying to scare you

away," Klint said. "I was trying to provide a good ghost story for your uncle's book. Perhaps you'll think I was using him for my own benefit, but few people can resist an escape story. And an escape from a ghost — well, what more could a reader ask? I felt that many people would read your uncle's travel book, and the better the book the more tourists it would attract to the Caymans."

"I see," Linda said after a pause. "But you said you had another reason. What was that?"

"To be honest, I did hope the ghost scene might frighten Mars away from the coral beds. I didn't even want him to know about black coral, and I hated for him to find the beds and actually retrieve black coral from them."

"Wouldn't that be good advertising for your islands? A unique sort of thing like that?"

"There are drawbacks to every idea," Klint said. "Sure I want tourists to come, but I don't want to see them make the black coral beds a thing of the past. And that could happen. Those beds *are* unique. And Mars probably told you that there's a world of coral down there. It's true. But it's estimated that it takes ten years for a coral bed to replenish itself. Before we can open those beds to hordes of tourists, we'll need some conservation laws."

"I see," Linda said, warming toward Klint.

"Mars was moving too fast for me. You've probably guessed by now that I stole the coral he brought up. Me-first guys like him are a danger to ecology. But to get back to the ghost story. I paid Taurus to play pirate for me. When he finished his act, he hid the costume aboard the *Tortuga*, never thinking that he'd be going out again this season. We both forgot about it."

"You've given me a lot to think about," Linda said. "I'm trying not to judge you, and trying even harder not to misjudge you. That's why I've treated you so coolly on this voyage. Don't think I didn't feel guilt pangs when you risked your life to save mine this afternoon. You could have been washed overboard."

"If I'd gone over, you would have gone, too. At least we would have been together. I believe that's called irony."

Linda rose and kissed Klint, and they were locked in an embrace for a long time. Then with a parting good-night kiss Linda left him and went into the deckhouse. Not wanting to disturb Virgie or Gem, she turned on no lamp, but she had hardly been inside a moment when she heard a light tapping on the door.

"Mars," Linda whispered, "you can't come in here. Virgie and Gem are sleeping."

"Then you come out. I have to talk to you."

Linda joined Mars on deck. He hunched his shoulders and led with his head in the old familiar way as they strolled to the rail.

"I've been planning how I'll polish that coral," Mars said, ignoring the subject of the recent storm as if it had never happened.

"Mars, what happened to you during the squall? I was afraid you'd been washed overboard."

"Not me," Mars said. "I was safe and sound down in the hold. It got damp down there. Needed more action on the bilge pump, but I kept my feet dry. Where were you?"

"Oh, I was around," Linda said lightly.

"I'm planning a black coral ring for myself," Mars said, "and I thought you'd like one, too. An engagement ring, for instance. It would be different. Everyone would be talking about Mars Ramsey's girl and her black coral engagement ring. How about it? What do you say? I may go into the black coral business. A guy could make a mint with it. That stuff is dynamite, and I'd have a corner on the market. What do you say, Linda?"

"I'll have to say no, Mars," Linda said gently. "We're no good for each other. You have such high hopes that I could never live up to them. With me you would always live with a sense of disappointment. There's the right girl for you somewhere. You'll find her, and when you do, you'll be glad you didn't get stuck with me."

"If you say 'Can't we just be friends?' I'll flip."

"Then I won't say it. A clean break will be the least painful way of parting for both of us." She tried to think of something else to say, but in the next moment Mars had gone.

Linda sat on deck for a long time that night dreaming of what it would be like to be Klint's wife. Without in the least knowing it, he had helped her make her decision when he had referred to Mars as a me-first guy. He hadn't spoken with vindictiveness or jealousy. He had merely spoken the truth.

Mars was a me-first guy. During the storm he had been a hider instead of a helper. He was brilliant and charming, but all babies are charming. And Mars was like a baby, totally absorbed by his own fingers and toes. Now Linda could see that his childlike innocence was more a childish callowness.

On the other hand, Klint had taken on a new dimension. He no longer seemed like a Roman Caesar cut on a gold coin, but rather like the ruler of her heart. Klint excited her, yet he had a mature stability. His kindliness and tranquility would be easy to live with. His deep interest in everyone and everything would keep their lives exciting, and she knew that because of his inborn secretiveness, their marriage would have an aura of mystery to it that they could enjoy solving together.

For the first time in her life Linda had conquered her own fears. She knew she could succeed as a staff nurse, a private nurse, a wife, or a combination of all three. And now she saw a pattern to her life. It was as if an unseen hand were guiding her, yet leaving the important choices to her wisdom. She felt as if in finding Klint she had discovered a reason for her existence. She could see the design in everything that had happened to her in the past few months, and she basked in the warmth of her insight.

She had made her decision.

We hope you have enjoyed this Large Print Edition. Other Thorndike, Wheeler or Chivers Press Large Print books are available at your library or directly from the publishers.

For more information about current and up-coming titles, please call or write, without obligation, to:

Publisher
Thorndike Press
295 Kennedy Memorial Drive
Waterville, ME   04901
Tel. (800) 223-1244

Or visit our Web site at:
www.gale.com/thorndike
www.gale.com/wheeler

OR

Chivers Large Print
published by BBC Audiobooks Ltd
St James House, The Square
Lower Bristol Road
Bath BA2 3SB
England
Tel. +44(0) 800 136919
email: bbcaudiobooks@bbc.co.uk
www.bbcaudiobooks.co.uk

All our Large Print titles are designed for easy reading, and all our books are made to last.